Line Drive to Love

ANGEL JENDRICK

JAMES LORIMER & COMPANY LTD., PUBLISHERS
TORONTO

James Lorimer & Company Ltd., Publishers acknowledges funding support from the Ontario Arts Council (OAC), an agency of the Government of Ontario. We acknowledge the support of the Canada Council for the Arts. This project has been made possible in part by the Government of Canada and with the support of Ontario Creates.

Cover design: Tyler Cleroux
Cover image: Kate Phillips

Library and Archives Canada Cataloguing in Publication

Title: Line drive to love / Angel Jendrick.
Names: Jendrick, Angel, author.
Series: RealLove.
Description: Series statement: Real love
Identifiers: Canadiana 20240394992 | ISBN 9781459419599 (hardcover) |
    ISBN 9781459419582 (softcover)
Subjects: LCGFT: Novels.
Classification: LCC PS8619.E52 L56 2024 | DDC jC813/.6—dc23

Published by:
James Lorimer &
Company Ltd., Publishers
117 Peter Street, Suite 304
Toronto, ON, Canada
M5V 0M3
www.lorimer.ca

Distributed in Canada by:
Formac Lorimer Books
5502 Atlantic Street
Halifax, NS, Canada
B3H 1G4
www.formaclorimerbooks.ca

Distributed in the US by:
Lerner Publisher Services
241 1st Ave. N.
Minneapolis, MN, USA
55401
www.lernerbooks.com

Printed and bound in Canada.

For Coach C.

Thank you for all the hard work you've put in, on and off the field. Players like Rory need coaches like you!

01 Baseline

IT'S DO-OR-DIE TIME.

Drawing in a breath, I quickly scan the runners on base as I step back up to the home plate. Jaya's leaning heavily on second like she's ready to steal third, and the newbie, Ava, is picking at her nails on first. Her lack of attention to the game has me wincing, like shivers down my spine whenever one of my vinyl records skips.

I shrug it off and exhale, rolling my shoulders

before getting into position again. The pitcher and I make eye contact, and for a moment, all other distractions melt away. It's just her and me now, having a little showdown on the field like we've done hundreds of times over the years.

"C'mon, Rory, you got this! Let's go Hot Sparks!"

I don't need to look; I'd know Jaya's voice anywhere, and my lips twitch from the encouragement. I widen my stance and brace for Sophie Mitchell's oncoming pitch, anticipating that it'll fall short again. The game has been long and dragged-out, and she's been getting sloppier the last couple of innings. My coach would have yanked me off the field by now.

Give it up, bro. Coach C's not your coach anymore.

I grit my teeth and shake my head, willing the thought away, but the memory of the loss lingers just enough to throw me off balance and have me doubt myself at the last second. I notice the pitch too late, swinging at nothing but air.

"STRIKE TWO!" the umpire booms from behind me.

Focus, Taylor.

Taking another deep breath, I step outside of the home plate once more and shake my hands and arms loose. My palms are damp inside my gloves, and there is a trickle of sweat dripping down my back.

There's no rush, Ror, take the time you need to do it right.

My dad's advice from over the years comes back to me, and I almost smile. I start to look for Mom and him in the stands but quickly reprimand myself. They're not here tonight; of course they're not.

I exhale in a rush, relaxing the tension in my shoulders and return to the plate.

"Hey, batter batter!"

"C'mon Rory! Show 'em how it's done!"

The shouting from both teams fades away as I get back into position, and when the familiar slick of sweat soaks the hairline around my neck, I'm glad my Buff headband halts most of it from my forehead.

My gaze tunnels down the line at my opponent in wait. Mitchell makes the pitch, and on instinct, my hands squeeze the handle of my bat as I anticipate the impact seconds before the swing.

Crack!

"Yes!" Jaya crows.

The moment the ball connects, I'm running down the baseline like my ass is in mortal danger. The early summer breeze whips at my cheeks as I barrel toward first, and as I zero in on my teammate still lounging about, there is a millisecond or more where time slows and I just enjoy the pulse thudding in my ears. Then I growl out, "Get moving, Ava!"

The new girl perks up at the sound of her name, and her eyes widen as she notices me. Then she takes off like a bat out of hell. I make a mad dive for first, *literally*, and the packed earth rushes up to greet me as I skid my torso across the ground. By some miracle, my fingertips graze the base.

"SAFE!"

I pull myself to my feet, swiping sweat and dirt off my throat and look around for Ava.

"Go, Ror!" Jaya again, but then I hear others on my team calling out similar things.

"I don't know how she managed that." The first base player shakes her head, following my gaze to where Ava is gasping for breath on second. She's grinning like she didn't just almost cost us the game, and I roll my eyes.

"Me neither."

I bend my knees a little, getting ready for the next pitch. Char, one of our strongest hitters, is up to bat, and she drives the ball out to left field on the first try. "Move, move!" I cry to Ava, taking off to second. My heart is thumping as I run, noting that both Jaya and Ava cross home plate. I hold on third once I see the ball whiz past.

"What was the hesitation out there, Taylor?" Coach quizzes when I finally make it back to the dugout. He pulls me aside, away from the team's earshot and crosses his arms over. Coach Dan is a prick, but in the last few years, I've learned to curb my temper around him. His daughter, on the other hand . . .

"Sorry, Coach, I don't know what came over

me." I mumble, pulling my helmet off. Blonde bangs had escaped my headband so I take that off too. He's frowning at my undercut in exactly the same way he's done since I chopped off my long hair last year — like I'm ruining the stereotypical girl softball look if I'm not sporting a ponytail or braid.

Whatever.

Shrugging past him, I rush to where my stuff sits and have just enough time for a drink before it's time to head back onto the field. Neallie shoots me a glare as I pass her on the pitcher's mound, and I have to bite my tongue to hold back any retort. Between her endless remarks and the coach's lack of support, I should have quit the team a dozen times over by now. Except I don't, because quitting is for losers.

I *will* take the Hot Sparks to the championships this summer. No one else has what it takes to get the team there. Afterwards, I'll earn my old position back on the provincial team before I drop Coach Dan once and for all.

No matter what it takes.

02 Behind the Line

Jaya's mom pulls up in front of my Summerside house, parking behind my parents' wheelchair-accessible van. The pit of my stomach churns as I glance out the window at the old, narrow two-storey I grew up in, observing the errant weeds taking over the small garden beneath the two front windows. It's been a while since I tidied them, and by the look of the lawn, I'll need to cut it again soon. My chest tightens in the most uncomfortable way, and I rub at it absently before grasping the door handle.

"Thanks for the lift." Shouldering my bag, I offer Jaya and her mom a half-hearted wave before exiting their SUV.

"You and Jay played a great game tonight!" Jaya's mom calls from the open window, and I turn in time to catch her smile. Jaya and her family have helped a lot over the past two years.

"Thanks, Mrs. Williams. Did you get any of it on video?"

"She did you one better," Jaya grins, leaning out the window, her eyes two big chocolate pools as they knowingly study me. "Mom went live with the game. Your parents saw the whole thing!"

Going live. Why didn't I think of that? My vision blurs as tears threaten and I swallow, backing up as I bob my head up and down like some kind of over-enthusiastic puppy, "That's so great, thank you. I bet Dad appreciated it." I rasp, swivelling around before anyone sees the tear slip out. "Gotta go, see ya!"

Tossing my arm up in an awkward, over-the-shoulder wave, I make a cowardly retreat up the driveway.

The house is quiet when I enter, but for the low hum of the ventilator in the next room. I set my bag quietly on the floor, sliding it under the bench Dad built years ago for the hallway. As I remove my cleats, an invisible weight piles onto my shoulders, a shameful part of me wanting to turn around again and leave. I pull my phone out — if nothing else, at least it'll stall the inevitable.

I could hit my best friend up. Carlos lives two streets over and would open the door, no questions asked. He knows what I'm like when I get like this — like the weight of the world is on top of me.

An incoming snap breaks my train-wreck ideas, and I click into Jaya's message.

My cuz got in yesterday. Gonna see if she wants to go for a dip tmr with me and Sky before practice. You in?

I squint at the message before politely declining. I'd forgotten her cousin from the west coast was visiting, but if she wasn't, it wouldn't change my answer. Between work, ball, and home, I have zero free time.

"Rory, that you?" A soft voice chimes from the next room, and I halt whatever else I was going to do with my phone. Leaving it alone on the bench, I make my way to the den in my sock feet. I'm still wearing my dirty softball uniform, but it's become routine to see him like this.

"Hey, Ma," I whisper as I enter, closing the sliding door after me. Mom has her head tucked into her shoulders as she examines the thousand-piece puzzle she's currently working on. The only light on in the room is the lamp over her table, and I glance to where Dad is restlessly dozing. The hospital bed is in a half recline, and Mom must have added more blankets in the few hours I was gone. My dad doesn't stay up late too often these days.

"Heard you guys watched the game," I murmur, crossing the room to Mom. I bend to kiss her cheek, before pulling out the chair opposite hers.

Her smile is wide and so vibrant, so *youthful*, that it's hard to believe she's almost sixty. As my parents like to call it, I was a "happy accident." My brother and sister were already eighteen and twenty when Mom discovered she was pregnant.

"Right to the end. You guys won by five! Congratulations."

"Thanks. Did Dad see it too?" I can't explain it, but I need him to see me play. Making him proud of me, of what I can accomplish, before . . . before . . .

I blink, shaking the thought away.

Mom nods and smiles again. "He did. He just fell asleep not too long ago."

Nodding too, I dare another glance at my old man. That pestering, constrictive sensation in my chest is back, and I jump up from the table. Needing to move, I head to my parents' vinyl record collection, skimming my index finger over albums I grew up listening to. Van Morrison, Janis Joplin, Elvis, and Johnny Cash, to name a few. Until recently, there was hardly a time when it was quiet in the house, as there always seemed to be a record playing.

When my finger pauses on one of my favourites, the

1968 album by the Mamas & the Papas, I'm breathing like I've run twenty minutes on the treadmill. I lift it off the shelf, slipping the vinyl from its case and into the player. I've heard this album a million times, so it doesn't take much guesswork to get the needle just right. Seconds later, the soft intro melody in "Dream a Little Dream of Me" begins.

Nothing in the world soothes the soul quite like music.

"Rory?"

I silently backtrack to Mom and offer my hand, "Dance with me?"

"Oh, honey," she whispers, and I can tell by the way her lips purse that she's dying to ask too many questions and then console me when I finally break. Thankfully, she does none of that and instead, takes my hand in hers.

And we dance.

03 Team Spirit

"THE SHIT I DO FOR YOU," Carlos pants, running alongside me on the Water Street boardwalk. I might be biased since I grew up here, but I think Summerside, PEI, is the perfect definition of beautiful, smaller city life. Everything we need is at our fingertips without sacrificing tourist attractions like the boardwalk and pier. I love it down here, so close to the salt water you can almost taste it. On nice, clear summer mornings, people in kayaks and yachts are already out on the water. When I'm here alone, the peacefulness grounds me in ways I can't explain.

"You didn't have to come."

Carlos snorts, side-glancing me with those deep brown eyes, "Bro, it's the only way I see you during softball season. You'd think you played for —" his sentence dies in his throat, his lips clamping shut, but I know exactly what he was about to say.

You'd think you played for the Whitecaps again.

Gritting my teeth, I pump my legs to go faster. We've made the six-kilometre trek from one end of the boardwalk to the other, and I can see the tip of the new resort coming into view.

"My bad, I know it's a sore topic for you," Carlos grimaces, swiping the back of one dark hand across his sweaty brow.

Sore is an understatement. I used to be one of the leading pitchers on the most respected softball team on the island — until a stunt at the skate park had me laid up due to a broken fibula. For the rest of the softball season, I watched from the sidelines as Neallie — who used to warm the bench — replaced me. The *same* Neallie I stupidly crushed on through all of sixth grade and into the seventh. The *same* Neallie who never liked me because I acted too much like a "boy" in her eyes. She replaced me on the team, and by the time tryouts for the next season rolled around, my cast was newly off and I was too out of shape to make the U19 provincial team. So *yeah*, I was bitter alright.

"It's okay, I'll just need to be more careful this summer." I slow to a walk, cracking a faint grin as I catch my breath. "No more half pipes 'til winter."

With each step through the wooded area of the trail, ducks squawk in the nearby marsh. It's so peaceful, and I love that there are birdhouses hanging all over the forest.

"Or not even then, if you'll be training year-round." Carlos deadpans, a long exhale blowing a runaway dreadlock from his face.

"How's Pascal doing with the lifeguard job?"

Carlos shrugs, "No complaints, except that she doesn't see me enough."

That has me smirking, and I give him a nudge, "Your girlfriend has separation anxiety, bro. She'd live in your back pocket if she could."

"Jealous?"

"Hell, no. Too much work," I huff out a laugh. *Well, I walked right into that one.* "At least with softball, it might get me to college!"

My dream has always been to play at the college level and have my parents cheering me on in the stands. Playing for the Whitecaps again will get me closer to that goal. Of course, growing up in a lower income bracket than most — or at least annoying girls like Neallie — there won't be a free ride waiting for me when I graduate. *Unless* I get that scholarship.

I have my whole life to find The One and have a Johnny and June romance. This moment right here?

It's just for me.

"Let's hustle, ladies!" Coach Dan barks that evening at practice, giving the team wide berth as he slowly

 LINE DRIVE TO LOVE

circles the outfield. He's always been a hardass, but I smirk when a few of the newer, less committed players groan. It doesn't matter that we've been doing this for an hour already or that my legs are burning from overuse; the ball field is where I find my Zen. Besides, I've got an AirPod in one ear with all my favourite oldies playing to hype me up.

Coach Dan wants more hustle? *No problemo.*

"What's with the stupid grin?" Jaya feigns a glare my way, but we pick up the pace, my toes almost touching her heel as we shuffle around the field.

"What, you mean this?" My smile widens, and I start singing along to "Ain't No Mountain High Enough" by Marvin Gaye and Tammi Terrell. Jaya laughs as I belt out the second verse, but she and my other friend, Sky, are joining in by the time the chorus approaches.

"Rory Taylor! What'd I tell you about singing at practice?" The coach glares from his place near the pitcher's mound.

"Uhh . . . that it's crucial for team spirit?" my

question comes out innocently, as if I haven't heard it all before.

Sky snorts, always one of the first to have my back. She's been my friend for years, the same as Jaya and Carlos, and we even dated for a few weeks in grade nine. It didn't take us long to discover we were better off as friends.

"That your singing sucks?" Neallie tuts back, falling out of formation to pull her long black hair over her shoulder. Her prissy attitude sets my teeth on edge, so I straighten as well, taking off to the infield.

The coach switches things up — working with me, for once, instead of against — and tells everyone to grab their gloves. Sky joins me back in the outfield, where we practice catching for a while, when a curly cascade of the thickest, richest black hair catches my eye through the fence. My gaze lands on soft skin the colour of nutmeg, before falling to a pair of snug jeans that accentuate a curvy body. For a fleeting moment it's as if time stands still. I forget what I'm doing, instead tracking those curls all the way to the bleachers.

"Ror, heads-up!"

The warning comes seconds before the softball plows into my stomach, pushing all the air from my lungs. "Ugh." I keel over, wheezing.

"Rory, you okay?" Sky's beside me now, hand on my shoulder, but I wave her off.

"I'm fine." As embarrassment burns my cheeks, I'm already looking around for the girl with the gorgeous hair. Even from across the field, I spot her, perched on the third row of the bleachers with a notebook in her hands.

"Who is that?"

Sky squints down the field, taking in the newcomer. "Jaya's cousin. C'mon, we're doing base work now."

Following Sky to the infield, I can hardly take my eyes off the girl in the bleachers, and the closer I come to her noticing me, the quicker my heart beats.

Dude, what is wrong with you?

As soon as practice is over, I'm the first one packed and off the field. Something compels me to

Jaya's cousin, and I hike up to where she's still busily writing in her notebook.

My gaze follows the elegant swipe of her pen and then back up, running along her arm and shoulder, to the side of her face. Her eyes are hidden behind a pair of large framed beige and blue glasses, and butterflies erupt in my stomach at the thought of her looking at me.

Hold up. Say what?

Hell no. That's where it starts, and I *so* don't have the time for a crush.

I turn to leave, but Jaya and Sky are climbing the bleachers to us. "I see you've met," Jaya states, thumping down beside her cousin. The girl startles, lifting her gaze to find the three of us in her bubble, her brown eyes, almost identical to Jaya's, widening.

"Sorry, I was completely in the zone," she says, pulling out a pair of her own AirPods by way of explanation.

"Oh, so you haven't met Rory?"

I lift my hand in an awkward wave, willing my

racing heart to slow. Gone is the confident softball player. Now it's like I've lost the ability to speak or think. Am I blushing? *So embarrassing.* "Hi."

"Hi, I'm Shanti." A shy smile appears, and her less than discreet appraisal of my appearance makes me all too aware that I'm still in my filthy uniform.

"Ready, cuz?"

"Yep," Shanti gathers her things, offering me another smile, "It was nice meeting you, Rory."

I say nothing. I'm frozen. It's not until they leave and Sky swats me hard in the arm that I snap out of it.

"What just happened?"

Sky laughs, throwing her arm around my shoulders, "That, my friend, was some serious gay panic."

04 Dugout Duels

I DON'T REMEMBER THE WALK HOME that night, or the visit with my dad before heading to bed. I do remember not sleeping, with thoughts and images of Shanti filling my exhausted brain until her name became a silent chant to my desperate, deprived lesbianism. Now, two days later, not much has changed except that I'm cranky from the lack of sleep and super annoyed at myself for doing exactly what I promised myself I wouldn't.

Obsessing over a girl.

"What's going on out there, ladies? Where's the focus?" The coach's hands go up in a flurry of frustrated gestures as he drills us from the dugout, and I duck my head. My temper is simmering as it's been for the better part of the game, and Neallie's lousy pitching isn't helping. "It's the top of the fifth, and we're still down by four. You've got two innings left to show the Riptides what we're made of."

"Let me pitch."

My plea surprises everyone, not just me, as I've laid down and taken the low-key bullying and favouritism for so long now. Jaya and Sky stare wide-eyed at me, but I stand my ground and ignore Neallie's glare. My gaze lands on Coach Dan's. "Please, Coach, let me pitch."

He looks torn at the offer — admittedly, more than I'd hoped for. He knows I'm the best choice, but will he pull his own daughter from the game?

"Not on your life, Taylor. This is my game," Neallie slams her water bottle down and snatches her glove up.

My hands go up in a "calm down" gesture. "Sure, but putting me in —"

"We don't have time to switch things up," Coach Dan interrupts, a slight grimace accompanying the letdown. "Get back out there team and do your best."

Whoops and hollers ring out as the team jogs out to the field. I'm more reserved, my bitterness threatening to take over. I glance down to see the slight tremble of my hands and shove my left into my glove.

Neallie knocks my shoulder as she walks past, turning to give me a smirk. She'd be pretty if she wasn't so evil. The thought of Shanti's shy smile temporarily steals my focus, and I shake it away. As much as I wouldn't mind her living rent-free in my head for a while, it can't happen.

"You just wish you were good with the ball. Just like you wish you were a boy. No one cares, Rory." Neallie laughs, coming so close we're almost chest to chest. I can smell the blend of sweat and perfume coating her golden skin as she sneers, "Forgettable. That's what you are."

My skin flushes, and several parts of me tremble at once. I clench and unclench my free hand, a vision of punching her as clear as day in my mind. I move in closer, threatening, looking around to see any witnesses only to discover our tiff is the main event.

"Don't listen to the haters, Ror. Be who you're meant to be, and the right people will flock to you."

My father's words pull me back to the moment, and I step back, releasing a breath. Fighting won't help me earn a spot on the provincial team.

"For being so forgettable," I finally say, backing up to head to my shortstop position, "you sure think about me a lot, Neallie."

Her growl has me laughing.

"So we lost, big deal. Not many club teams go undefeated."

I scowl into my iced tea, raising the glass for another sip. The ice has long since melted, and the room-temperature sweetness of the liquid reminds me how much I hate sweet tea. I glance around Jaya's busy backyard at my Hot Sparks teammates jumping in and out of the pool, before muttering to her, "You don't get it, Jay."

"Sure, I do. Neallie sucked tonight, but you weren't at your best either," Jaya gives me a knowing look, a coy smile tugging the corners of her mouth. "Shanti on your mind?"

I groan, burying my face in my hands and ignoring her ensuing laughter, "Sky told you?"

"Rory, Rory," Jaya pats my back, still chuckling, "You forget I've known you since our t-ball days. You lit up like a Christmas tree when Shanti said hi."

"No way! You're making that up." Now I'm laughing, my chest and stomach relaxing in response, and I forget about the game. Sky waves us over from where she's leaning against the pool wall, droplets of water dripping off her russet brown hair.

"Wanna swim?" Jaya asks me, already standing.

"Yeah, just give me a sec," I murmur, already typing a message out to my mom.

"Checking in?"

"Uh-huh. Pa had a rocky day, so . . ." I trail off when a new text pops up.

Ma: All good here, Ror. Have fun! Xxo

Me: KK lemme know if that changes. Xxo

I sigh in relief, placing my phone down and flashing Jaya a grin. "Ready."

We strip down to our bathing suits, Jaya in a bikini and me in my sports bra and beach shorts, before heading in with Sky. I'm the only openly queer person on the Hot Sparks — Sky still has one foot in the closet — so I'm used to the looks I get from some of my teammates. Not mean or anything, more like . . . curious, like I'm an exotic animal they might want to explore.

We splash and fool around, picking up a game of Nerf ball with Ava and Bea, but I keep glancing around, disappointed when Shanti doesn't show. I don't know why I thought she'd come tonight, considering it's a team party, but I'd be lying if I said it wasn't the sole reason for my decision to go. As Dad's condition worsens, I prefer to stay close, but Mom encouraged me to come to Jaya's.

"There you are! I didn't think you'd make it." Jaya called, waving to someone over my shoulder.

I turn and my legs get so weak I immediately grab the pool's ledge. Shanti's hovering outside the door to the house, looking extremely out of place in a thin long-sleeve and leggings. Her bouncy curls topple midway down her back, and my mouth dries up as she looks my way.

"I thought you were having a bonfire," Shanti replies, glancing down at her clothes.

"Oops sorry, Shanti, I forgot to text you the change. That's okay!" Jaya wades over to the ladder, "I'm sure I have something you can put on."

"I don't think it'll fit her," Ava whisper-yells, and I shoot her a death glare.

"Shut up, newbie."

Shanti is beautiful and curvy, and I'll be damned to hear anything else. Sky and I follow Jaya out of the pool, grabbing our towels on the way to Shanti. "We could just hang out," I suggest, warming all over when Shanti eyes the muscled definition of my stomach. She flushes when she gets caught, but if what Jaya said is right, my appreciation should be obvious.

"How about me and Jay swim and you keep Shanti company?" Sky grins, giving me a slight shove toward Shanti.

"Oh, um . . ." Shanti peters off.

"'Kay, have fun kids!" Jaya, clearly understanding the assignment, drags Sky with her back to the pool.

It's just the two of us on the deck now, staring at each other. An awkward chuckle escapes me, and I gesture to the outdoor table set I was at before, "Wanna sit down?"

"Sure,"

"So, er, you're Jay's cousin?"

Shit, of all the questions . . . don't be such an idiot, Ror.

Shanti giggles, "You can't tell?"

"What? No, I . . ." I trail off, darting my gaze from her to Jaya, noting the difference in their complexions. They both have Asian ancestry — Indian and

Mongolian, I believe — and almost identical brown eyes, right down to the flare of mischief in them, but Shanti is curvier and her curls are tighter. I wonder what her father's lineage is, but instead of asking, I just shrug, "I can. I dunno why I said that, sorry."

"Are you nervous?" Shanti asks once my shirt is back on and I'm sitting beside her. She pushes her glasses up on her nose to peer up at me "I am."

"You're nervous?" I shift my chair closer to her, watching her hands and eyes. My dad always said you can tell a lot about a person by their body language, and sure enough, I see a slight tremble in Shanti as she clasps her hands together.

Her gaze falls from mine and another little smile appears, "I'm better with fictional people than real people." A peel of laughter rings out, and her hand flies up to cover her face. "I can't believe I just said that! *Books*. I read a lot of books."

"What do you read?" My heart skips a beat. I wanna know more — everything there is to know about Shanti Williams.

She tucks a curl behind her ear, biting her lip, and the urge to kiss her has me leaning forward in my seat. She doesn't notice. "Sapphic romance, mostly."

I nod like I know what she's talking about, mentally making a note to research that term later. "Favourite book?"

She smiles, and I love the way her eyes instantly light up, "*Annie on My Mind*, hands down. Do you read?"

I'm about to reply with something stupid, maybe like, *No, but I would for you*, when Neallie comes into view with Kamryn and Becky. "Dad's already sent out my recruitment video to coaches in the states. It sounds like I'll have my pick of colleges."

Her words are like a knife to the ribs, and I suck my teeth, the uncomfortable ache back in my chest. My stomach churns, the vibe in the room doing a one-eighty.

That's supposed to be me.

Breaking my leg screwed up all plans for the future. I'm heading into my senior year — what if it's too late to pursue my softball dream?

"Rory?"

"I need to leave," I announce, scraping my chair back. I take in the confusion on Shanti's face, my stomach rolling, "Wanna come?"

Shanti hesitates, and that's good enough for me. This was a mistake, anyway. I swallow, giving her a small wave, "Bye, Shanti."

Playing for the Same Team

"SEE YA NEXT WEEK, BUDDY!" I ruffle Jax's hair and watch as he bolts off the field to his mother. It's my second summer working for the city's recreation department, doing anything from mowing and chalking the sports fields to assisting with summer day camps and Active Start programs. Any job that keeps me close to the softball field is the one for me, and besides, I love getting the chance to introduce young kids to sports.

"Well, no one cried this time, so I'd say we did good," jokes Hunter, the first-year college student I'm paired with this summer. I force a laugh, helping to pack up the equipment and carry it across the field to his car.

I've been in a funk ever since Jay's party, one not even my usual sit-down with Dad early this morning helped. I usually read him the paper or we listen to a record together, but I can't let go of Neallie's bragging. Life is unfair, and bitches like her continually remind me of that fact. I've always had to work harder and longer than Neallie, and yet she's the one with a college guarantee.

"I was gonna ask if you have plans today, but looks like you do." I follow Hunter's gaze to the edge of the soccer field and spot Shanti watching us.

An indescribable warm feeling washes over me, genuine laughter bubbling to the surface, "Yeah, I just might. See ya, Hunter."

"Sorry to just show up. Jaya said you'd be here," Shanti gushes as I reach her side, looking anywhere but at me as she wrings her fingers together. She's wearing cute denim shorts and an Elvis t-shirt that instantly catches my attention. She's nervous, and the way she wrinkles her nose in thought is adorable. The need to push Shanti away yet pull her closer has me torn. How can I possibly fit her into my hectic life?

"*Annie on My Mind* is about lesbians," I blurt, for no reason *whatsoever*. I noticeably cringe, wishing I could go back in time and kick myself as Shanti appears to blush from the inside out. She looks absolutely *mortified*, probably because I practically yelled *lesbian* from the rooftops.

"I, uh, looked it up. Online," my voice sounds strangled, and I yank at the collar of my golf shirt.

We leave the fields of Credit Union Place and head in the direction of Gen X, the indoor skate park I hung out at growing up. The weather is hot and sticky, but somehow I still catch traces of Shanti's perfume. Or maybe it's deodorant? Whatever it is, she's making me dizzy. We're walking close but not touching, and more than once I almost take Shanti's hand. It feels natural to be around her, even if we're both a bit extra in the nerves department. I drink from my Gatorade, sneakily observing her from the corner of my eye.

"I take it you didn't know what I meant when I said I read sapphic romance?" Shanti finally asks. I pause, the word I had meant to research dawning on me, so I shake my head.

"Honestly, the most reading I do is the newspaper every morning." My shoulders slump a little.

"A newspaper? You mean on an eReader?"

I laugh, and when she wrinkles her nose a second time, that urge to hold her hand returns. I clench my fist at my side and shake my head, "No, a real paper. Jay calls me a hippie, but it's whatever. I like what I like, and get my love of old things from my parents. Now *they're* the hippies."

"Cute," Shanti replies, and when her finger accidentally grazes mine, I almost die. The action makes me stumble over my own damn feet on the sidewalk and I nearly face plant.

What is it about her? Why her? Why now?

"Do you mind walking me back to my grandparents?" Shanti asks, sounding amused. She's enjoying this, I just know it. "They own the bed and breakfast on —"

"— The corner of Spring and Fitzroy, yeah, I've been before. Nice place." I grimace, realizing what an impulsive ass I am. "Sorry, didn't mean to interrupt." I take a deep breath and let it out slowly, stopping to face Shanti. "Sorry, please continue."

Shanti wrinkles her nose, clearly trying not to laugh. She cuts her gaze to the ground, wringing her fingers nervously together. "There's something about you, Rory Taylor."

I hang on to her words, hoping she'll elaborate, but she doesn't. Not knowing whether she *likes* likes me is going to drive me batty, but I can't find the words to ask. And, it seems, neither can she.

That's fine, though. Some things aren't meant to be rushed.

"C'mon Ror, Mike, you know you wanna get in on this jive," Mom sings the following morning, Elvis's greatest hits playing in the background. Her hips sway as she twirls around the kitchen, her cooking apron on and wooden spoon pointed at us.

Shaking my head, I'm in awe of Mom's consistent positive mindset, even when one glance at my father would state the obvious. He lost function in his legs long ago. In fact, he needs to use a wheelchair, his remaining body functionality limited to partial use of his left hand and broken speech. The Eyegaze machine they received a month ago will be a lifesaver when Dad gets the hang of it, but honestly, if it wasn't for the endless spirit and humour from both of them, I don't know how we'd all be coping right now.

"I suppose we can't leave you hanging," I reply, flashing a grin Dad's way. He's strapped into his wheelchair, but there's no mistaking the joy in his blue eyes. "Can we, Pops?"

"N-noo, Whoawee." He's no longer able to pronounce his *Rs*. I jump up to unlock his chair, and I wheel him closer to Mom just as the next song begins. "That's All Right" belts from the record player, and with us each holding one of Dad's hands, Mom and I do a sloppy two-step around the kitchen.

I'll never forget these mornings. They look different than they did two years ago, but maybe that's what makes them so precious.

We dance to one more song before settling in for breakfast. I feed Dad small spoonfuls of applesauce as Mom finishes making French toast. I have to be careful because it doesn't take much for him to choke.

"Oof, sorry," I say softly, grabbing the napkin to dab his chin where applesauce spilled. It's getting harder for him. They think I don't know it'll be a feeding tube next.

Mom slides a plate of breakfast in front of me, bending to smooch a kiss on my forehead. She ruffles my hair, "Eat, love."

A small grin appears. "Thanks for breakfast, Ma."

"Of course." Mom reaches for Dad's applesauce, silently taking the task over and indicating I should eat.

She watches me curiously.

"What?"

"Something's different. I'm trying to figure out what." She angles her head and squints, like she'll suddenly develop x-ray vision. "What happened last night?"

"Nothing, usual practice." I give a noncommittal shrug before shoving more breakfast in, avoiding her gaze as I chew and knowing damn well she's onto me. There isn't much I can keep from her and Dad.

"Uh-huh. Meet anyone new?"

See?

My cheeks burn, and with my fair complexion, I'm no doubt blushing right down to my throat. Mom's keyed up, laughing now, as she knows she's got me. "Aha, I knew it! Who is she?"

"Jaya's cousin from Vancouver." The admittance comes easily, as if my heart has already made its mind up about Shanti. It's my brain not fully on board, and thoughts of Shanti come with a nagging clarity.

Liking her comes with a cost.

Benching the thought for now, I fill my parents in on meeting Shanti. I spent a good hour with her yesterday after I conveniently got us lost on the way back to her grandparents' bed and breakfast. We learned quite a bit about each other, each fact further cementing my out-of-control infatuation.

"She's cleaning rooms this summer, but free most mornings." I glance between my parents, chewing the inside of my cheek and add, "She likes to run. Thought maybe I'd see if she wants to join me sometime."

"This is exciting, Ror," Mom exclaims, reaching for Dad's hand this time. "We're happy for you, aren't we, Mike?"

"Whoawee is . . . going up," Dad agrees.

"Well, nothing's happened yet. I don't even know if she likes me." My blush continues, and I stare at my plate. I suspect Shanti does, but she hasn't come right out and said so.

The doorbell rings seconds before Carlos calls from the hall, "Morning!"

"Carlos, you're just in time for breakfast, come in!"

"No, he's not. We're finished," I mutter, but Mom ignores me, switching to autopilot as Carlos enters the kitchen. She jumps to grab him a plate, and I just shake my head at my friend. "Dude, I hope you came with an empty stomach."

"Always," Carlos grins, patting his flat abdomen. He gives my mom and dad a hug before sitting next to me. "So, what'd I miss?"

06 Practice Makes the Pitcher

"I COULD BE SNEAKING a beer at the festival right now."

I dig my cleats into the pitcher's mound, staring down the line at where Jaya is crouching in her catcher's position. Although it's just the two of us practising, we're in full gear, and I can still see Jaya's mouth moving behind her mask.

"Just sayin'."

"And risk your dad seeing?" I smirk at her bluff. She was all too eager to ditch her family today when I suggested an extra practice. Apparently, she's reached the age where going anywhere with parents is embarrassing, even if it's a tourist magnet like the Cavendish Beach Music Festival. Honestly, I'd be more embarrassed over the music than anything else. Totally wrong decade.

"Choose your number, Jay."

"All business, always." She whines, but points two fingers toward the ground. I nod, poising my body for the pitch. My dominant leg explodes off the mound, my left leg drops forward, and then the ball is soaring from my fingertips and barrels straight into Jaya's mitt. I grin, loving the rush and power of a great pitch. I wanna dance on the mound, kiss that plate like it's mine again. I'm *more* than a substitute for Coach Dan whenever Neallie takes off for a provincial game. I should be starting. Shortstop is killer, don't get me wrong. I get to have eyes everywhere, but watching Neallie take pitching from me made me realize just how much I wanted it. More than playing shortstop, more than *anything*.

More than Shanti?

I grit my teeth, centring myself before making another pitch.

"You gonna call Shanti?" Jaya asks as we're leaving the field an hour later. Since I have to stick around and chalk the fields for an upcoming U10 game, I linger by her car as she gets in.

"I don't . . . she never gave me her number."

Jaya rolls her eyes, snatching my phone the moment I set it down to swap my cleats for sneakers. "I'm adding it to your contacts." Her fingers fly over the keyboard. When she finishes, she hands it over with a smile. "She likes you, you know, says you're cute and give off main character vibes. Also, that you look like Erika Linder. Whoever that is."

I drop my eyes to the ground, unsure what to say, but butterflies take flight in the pit of my stomach. "I don't have time for . . ." I trail off, shaking my head. I can't even say it.

"A life?" Jaya tsks. "You wanna wait 'til Shanti meets someone back home, or are you gonna show her now how great the two of you could be?"

I grimace, bending to pick up my bag. "Since when are you into the mushy shit?"

Jaya gives me a playful shove, "Stuff it, Taylor. I can be romantic."

I laugh, and as she drives away, I head back to the field to get my work over with.

I'm gonna do it. I'm gonna call Shanti.

The thought has me grinning from ear to ear.

Turns out calling a girl out of the blue isn't for inexperienced baby gays like me. I pace my tiny bedroom until I give in and try to text Shanti instead. Five attempts later, I finally shoot off:

Me: Hey, Rory here. Wanna hang out again?

And breathe.

Wasn't so hard, right?

Until she doesn't immediately text back. One minute goes by, then two. I pace again, not realizing until Mom is knocking on my open door. "Ror, did you forget about our hundred-year-old floorboards? Sounds like you're about to come through the ceiling."

Halting in my tracks, I raise my hand and wordlessly pass her the phone before rubbing at the tension along my neck. Mom reads the message before giving me a gentle smile. "Do you want to be friends with this girl or date her, Ror?"

I frown, "She knows I like her, so I wanna hang out, get to know her."

Mom shakes her head, perching at the foot of my bed, "You hang out with Jaya, Sky, and Carlos. You go out with Shanti. I know I'm old-fashioned, but if I was sixteen again, I'd be a bit confused right now."

Groaning, I collapse beside her on the bed, "Will you help me, Ma?"

"Baby, of course." She pats my hip. "Sit up, seriously, it's not that bad. You just need to reword what it is you want."

"Just like that, huh," I mutter, taking the phone again. My thumbs hover over the keyboard. Mom rubs my back, forever trying to comfort me, and I lean into the embrace.

"Ask how her day was and follow with your real question. Maybe add in that you enjoyed spending time together yesterday."

"'Kay." Expelling a long breath, I try again.

Me: How was your day? I had fun yesterday, did you maybe wanna do it again? We could go for a run and grab smoothies after.

"Much better," Mom ruffles my hair, getting to her feet. By the door, she says, "Don't forget Beth, Darcy, and the kids are coming for dinner tomorrow."

The mention of my sister's family brings forth a grin. I haven't seen them since they drove over from New Brunswick for Father's Day. "Wouldn't miss it, Ma."

She leaves, and it's not long after that I receive a reply from Shanti. I'm hella glad I'm already sitting as I rush to unlock the phone. I let out a whoop.

Shanti: My day was okay, getting better now. A run and smoothies sounds amazing. How about the morning? I just have to be back by ten.

Me: Perfect, can't wait.

I could probably light a dark room with the wattage of my smile right now, but I don't care. I fall back on my bed, eager for the morning. Running with Shanti will steal time from Carlos, but he'll understand.

Shanti and I text back and forth awhile more. She tells me about her latest book and what her grandparents are like. I talk about ball and my older siblings, not daring to touch on the deeper issues in my life.

I fall asleep thinking about her lips, wondering if she's ever been kissed. I've shared a few messy lip locks with Sky, but they certainly weren't worth remembering.

Perhaps I'm an overachiever, but man, I'd love to be Shanti's first.

07 Running Bases

SHANTI'S A FEW MINUTES LATE the following morning, and I chuckle when I see her drive past me. I continue my stretches, watching as she pulls in to the antique store a block away. She steps out of the car, looking around for a moment before pulling out her phone. A handful of seconds later, I get a text.

Shanti: I don't see you! LOL.

I grin, quickly typing back.

Me: I'll come to you. Look to your left.

I take off down the boardwalk, aware of Shanti's gaze on me, and am glad I don't trip over my feet this time. "Hey," I say when I reach her side, observing the black leggings and plain black t-shirt. It's a warm morning to wear that, but I just smile, happy to see her.

"Just to warn you, I won't look that graceful when I run," Shanti acknowledges, following me across the street again.

I flash her a grin, "You'll look good, trust me."

We fall into some easy stretching, me low-key checking Shanti out. She's uncomplicatedly pretty, full of natural beauty and a quiet gentleness I can't get enough of.

"Did you walk here?" Shanti glances around like she's searching for my car.

"I did. I only live three blocks —" I point in the general direction of my street, "that way, on North Market."

"That's nice and close for you."

We jog south on the boardwalk, toward the pier,

and it takes no time at all to discover Shanti might have stretched the truth when she said she was a runner.

"I . . . haven't had much time for exercise lately," she pants as we reach the Knot, the new beach bar nestled between the Sunset Room and a flower shop. A sheen of sweat dots her forehead, and even though I doubt she's ever run outside of a gym class, her attempt to impress me is absolutely adorable.

"The B&B must be busy." We slow down, and when the boardwalk cuts off we keep heading toward Samuel's coffee shop.

"It's insane! Full house every night. I swear some people come just for Grandpa's Sabbakki Rava Idli," Shanti jokes, darting a glance my way. A shy smile appears. "He's not huge in his Indian traditions except for food, so he'll cook a blend of Indian and North American breakfast for the guests."

The loud rumble of my stomach surprises us both, and my hand flies to cover it up as Shanti giggles. Unsurprised that the tips of my cheeks are hot, a flustered laugh slips out. "I'm so sorry, I swear it's got a mind of its own."

"We better get some food in that belly," Shanti jokes, her gaze dropping to my hand before darting forward again.

We're quite the pair; she's shy and I'm hella awkward.

"So, uh," I scratch my nose, my mind blanking as my earlier thought up and disappears. I'm grasping at straws here, trying to keep the conversation going. Playing ball is so much easier. If a ball plows down the line between second and third I scoop it up and throw it to first. I know what to expect on the field, but dating? Or maybe dating? Sheesh. "Who's Erika Linder?"

"Jaya told you?" Shanti squeaks, and I laugh when she covers her eyes. "Ugh, kill me now."

We stop just before Samuel's, and I rock back on my heels, thoroughly enjoying her blush. "She also said you think I'm cute."

"So embarrassing," Shanti mutters, but when she bats those eyes my way, a smile teases the corners of her mouth. "Erika is a Swedish androgynous model and actress. You could be her twin, at least during her short-hair era. Blonde hair, blue eyes, jawline, clothing style," Shanti shrugs, and I love that she doesn't back down or shy away from what she wants to say.

I glance down at my muscle shirt and men's athletic shorts. I've never liked shopping in the women's section. If it was up to me, there would be a long lineup of gender-neutral clothing in every store. "Jawline?"

"Now you're just fishing for compliments." Shanti rolls her eyes, but she's laughing at me.

I'm grinning as we head into Samuel's, feeling lighter than I have in months. Being around Shanti does that for me. After watching my dad grab the check for years, I'm already tapping my debit card before Shanti has her change counted.

"I wasn't expecting that, but thank you," she says as we make our way to the two-seater table against the window that faces Water Street.

"Yeah, of course. No problem."

We sip our smoothies for a while, not speaking, but unless I'm delusional, the wide openness of

Shanti's eyes as we take turns sneaking in glances has a language all its own. It makes me nervous — *she* makes me nervous, and I suck in a breath, coughing when my smoothie goes down wrong. "S-so what were you writing the day we met?" I stammer between wheezing.

Surprisingly, out of all the questions she's answered so far, this is the one that has Shanti lowering her eyes and probably wishing she could disappear. The flip from flirty to fearful gives me whiplash, and I watch in amazement as she plays with her straw for a moment. "Not much, just a little story I'm working on."

My eyebrows shoot up, and I lean forward. "For real? That's so cool. What do you write? Just by hand or do you use a laptop, too?" I have so many questions, and thankfully, once Shanti realizes I'm genuinely curious she eagerly spills.

Her story sounds more like a full-length novel, but what do I know? So long as Shanti is happy, her voice full of passion as she gives me a detailed run-down of her dystopian romance, I could listen to her all day every day. It's crazy how life goes. How did I go from having tunnel vision when it came to softball, to wanting Shanti to narrate her book aloud just so I could hear this version of her?

08

Away Game

ON MONDAY, Dad is well enough that Mom drives us the hour to my away game just past Charlottetown. We're playing the Stratford Stealers, a team we've gone neck to neck in games with before. They're a solid team, their pitcher on point every inning, and I can't wait for the challenge. I talk non-stop on the drive, filling my parents in on softball news and Shanti. As much as he can, Dad low-key teases me about my crush yet encourages me to invite Shanti over. He's always been my biggest fan and best friend.

"I've got him," I wave Mom off, double checking that Dad is buckled before turning on his motorized wheelchair. I drop a kiss to his forehead, "Let's go, old man. You gonna cheer me on tonight?" It's getting harder for him to steer it himself, so I keep close as he drives down the ramp.

"Alwaaays, champ," Dad forces out, but he looks ready for bed, not a two-hour softball game.

Shrugging off the guilt, I ramble on as we head over the gravel parking lot toward the bleachers. "Maybe Neallie's been stuck with a bad case of diarrhea and can't pitch tonight. One could hope, amirite?"

"Rory!" Mom chastises ahead of us, never one to speak bad about anyone, not even an unbearable arch-nemesis.

Chuckling, I pat my dad on the shoulder before guiding his wheelchair to the edge of the bleachers. "What? Pa thought it was funny, right, Pa?"

"Hey Rory, Mr. and Mrs. Taylor," Jaya greets us, sidling up beside us. My eyes widen when I notice

Shanti beside her, and just like that, I'm taken back to the day before. We talked for a good hour before she realized she was late for work. I'd offered to go and help, not ready to part ways so soon, but she'd politely declined.

"Hey," I reply, barely glancing Jaya's way before settling on Shanti again. "Hi, again."

Jaya jabs me in the arm good-naturedly. "Dude, we've gotta go warm up and don't have time for those lovey-dovey eyes."

Annnnd Shanti and I are blushing again. Sheesh. I clear my throat, "Shanti, these are my parents."

"Hi, it's nice to meet you both." Shanti shakes Mom's hand first, but the moment her gaze falls fully on Dad, her smile wobbles slightly.

For the first time in two days, the tightness in my chest returns. I tear my gaze from Shanti and my parents and look out to the ball field, not looking at Jaya as I swallow, "Let's go."

"You okay?" Jaya asks, rushing to catch up as we head to the dugout.

I'm too upset to speak, so I just nod, digging my glove from my bag through the blur of tears. I get like this every time my parents come to see me play, and I hate it. I can't keep a lid on my emotions, and I swear, something always makes me cry. All it takes is one pitiful glance at the old man and I'm either pissed or heartbroken.

"What's happening? Ror lose her voice?" Sky jokes, coming up behind us.

"She's lost something, not sure it's her voice though."

Ignoring them, I head out to the field, digging out my phone and putting my AirPods in as I go. Moments later my favourite song by the Bee Gees, "Stayin' Alive," blasts through the earpieces. By the time the warm-up is over and the game begins, I'll be good and centred again.

Music is magic.

Neallie did *not* come down with the flu, so when we're entering the bottom of the seventh inning and the Stealers are up to bat, I'm crouched ready to go at shortstop. We're ahead by only one run, so it's crucial to keep the opposing team back. As I like to call it, it's do-or-die time out here on the field. They've been chanting all game, ruffling Neallie's feathers, and honestly, I'm surprised she's held on so well.

"Pitcher pitcher, what's the matter? Can't you pitch a lit-tle faster?"

"C'mon Neallie," I mutter, scanning the bases again. Jaya's been going strong all game behind the plate, even scrambling for a couple bunts and biffing them to first before the batter reached the base. Right now, there is only one opponent on second, number eleven, and she's crouched forward, ready to steal.

I suck in a breath as Neallie makes the pitch, noting straightaway it's wobbling wide on the right. My eyes narrow slightly as the ump calls it.

"Ball!"

The batter's count is 3–2 now. One more ball and they'll walk. That's a lot of pressure for a pitcher, and one glance at the way Neallie is clenching her free hand against her thigh tells me she's in agreement. *Enough of this.* It's time for a little gentle clapback.

Hopping from foot to foot, I holler, "*I turn the oldies on, and what do I hear?*"

Sky, all the way in left field, quickly shouts back, "*Your boy Elvis singing our cheer!*"

"*That's right!*" I sing-song, loud enough my parents can likely hear as I direct the rest of the chant to the Stealers. "*And we're gonna fight you, gonna fight you, gonna fight, fight 'til we win here tonight!*"

Neallie's next pitch is much better, and number eleven strikes out, but at the same time, the player currently on base steals third without Jaya getting them out in time. I curse, scowling when the Stealers begin their annoying chants once more.

"*She stole on you, she stole on you! While you were pickin' your nose . . .*"

"C'mon Hot Sparks, let's show 'em how we do it!" I shout over the racket, smacking my hand into my glove.

I don't know how, but we manage to fend off

anyone else getting to first. The game ends with a tie and a sense of accomplishment on both sides.

"Good game, good game," I say, shaking hands with each player on the Stealers as they walk past. I'm riding a high, and although I can't wait for a celebratory milkshake — a thing I do, win or lose, whenever my parents can get to my game — there's something I've gotta do first.

She's already waiting for me by the dugout, surprise and excitement gleaming in her luscious brown eyes as I near and she throws her arms around me. "That was amazing, Rory! You're really good!"

I freeze, unsure what to do in her arms. Do I return the embrace? When had we decided we were at the hugging stage?

"You never say that about me," Jaya whines a few feet away.

An uneasy laugh escapes me, and when I turn, the entire team is watching us closely. I realize Shanti's still holding me, and I break away, unable to look at her as I rub the back of my neck. "Sorry," I bite my lip, though a grin slips out. Taking a deep breath, I slip my hand in hers, and she legit startles from the contact. Her gaze shoots to mine, but rather than explain, I guide her away from the dugout, keeping our fingers intertwined as we walk toward the parking lot. Mom is already loading Dad into the van, so there's not much time left.

I glance at Shanti, silently studying her mood and gauging what she wants from this. My thumb grazes the back of her hand, my breath catching when our eyes meet. "Will you let me take you on a date?"

As soon as the question tumbles from my impulsive lips, doubt kicks in and a sickening churn starts in the pit of my stomach. If I could turn back time . . .

"So not a run and smoothies?" Shanti confirms with a teasing smile.

Chuckling, I shake my head, "A real date. I'll plan it." I don't know how we'll make this work, but I know I want to.

Shanti squeezes my hand, her cheeks rosy with delight, "I'd love to. Tell me when and where, and I'll be there."

I reluctantly let her hand go, but I'm grinning as I slowly back away, "I'll shoot you the time, but the details will be a surprise."

09

A Drill and a Date

I glare at Neallie's back Wednesday evening, in a foul mood ever since the coach called the extra practice. I should be romancing Shanti right now, giving her the best first date ever, not running laps around the field and doing base work. Any other time I'd be all for it, but since meeting Shanti, well, it almost feels like fate keeps getting in the way.

Up and down, up and down . . .

I blink the sweat from my eyes and chance a look

to the fence line. Shanti's in the bleachers with her notebook again and a pang of guilt hits me.

I shouldn't have asked her to come watch me.

It was an impulsive reaction to the date cancellation, though I never expected her to say yes. Watching Shanti now nose deep in her notebook, she must be wishing she'd said no.

"Watch it, Taylor!" Neallie barks when I get too close doing my Frankenstein kicks. She rubs her thigh and glares.

"My bad," I reply, but can't bring myself to feel even an ounce of sympathy. I sneak another glance at Shanti under the beak of my hat before pulling my attention back to practice.

The moment the coach blows his whistle I'm off the field, making my way to Shanti before Jay has a chance to interrupt us. She catches me climbing the bleachers and a grin appears, "Hi, Rory."

"Hi." And hell, I can't keep the stupid grin off my face either. My whole body comes alive around Shanti, like a flower does when the heat of the sun shines on its petals.

"Are you free tomorrow afternoon?" Besides cutting grass and chalking the soccer fields, I don't have much else going on. Luckily, I only work with the kids part-time.

Shanti scrunches her nose in thought before nodding. "Maybe by three or four, if I hustle with the checkouts."

"Okay, four it is. I'll pick you up." I take a seat beside her, close enough that my leg brushes hers, and breathe whatever fragrance she's been torturing me with since we met. She must not mind the stench of sweat and dill pickle sunflower seeds, because she's never complained about my less-than-stellar fragrance. Still, I make a mental note to buy some Listerine strips. "How's the story going? Did Isla make it past the blockade to Morgan yet?"

Looking at Shanti, you'd think she was writing a sweet romance, not a post–war zone dystopian book where every chapter ends on a cliffhanger and the main characters face nonstop life-and-death situations. I might not read, but I can tell she's got a gift.

"She made it past, only to discover Morgan was captured." Shanti quirks a smile, "Now Isla'll need to enlist the help of friends to save her."

"Tripp and Zaatar, right?"

"Hey, you remembered!" Shanti laughs, clearly pleased. I grin and give myself a figurative high-five.

A loud thump sounds on the bleachers, and both of us turn to see Sky and Jaya coming to join us. My shoulders slump a little, but it only makes me look forward to our date tomorrow even more.

"Hey, kiddo. All ready for your date night?" Mom asks as I rush into the kitchen. She's busy making another batch of energy balls for tomorrow's game, even though I've told her more than once it's unnecessary. She's got enough to worry about without adding baking to her list. She gives me an inquisitive look, one eyebrow arched up.

"Yep! Leaving now." I sidle up to give her a peck on the cheek and snatch an energy ball.

"I knew the moment I saw that vest at the thrift store it'd be perfect." Mom nods approvingly, smoothing her hand down the suede material and taking in my blue jeans and black skate shoes. She gives me a light squeeze around the shoulders. "Go. Get out of here. Have fun."

"I will. Love you, Ma."

"Love you too."

On the way to the front door, I grab the picnic backpack I found in the basement the other day. Dad's sleeping, or else I'd probably check in there too before heading out. A burst of nervousness bubbles in my stomach as I make my way to the two bikes sitting in my driveway. *What if Shanti thinks it's overkill?* I've never planned a date before. Half of me worries I'm too old-fashioned.

I pull my phone out, quickly finding my Spotify playlist and press play. The rich instrumentals of Carpenters' "Superstar" begins, and I let the timeless beauty of Karen's voice settle me as I grab the handles of the bikes and guide them down the street. I'd rather skateboard than ride a bike, but I didn't want Shanti to feel uncomfortable if I was skating beside her. The B&B is about a five-block hike, so walking both bikes is a bit of a balancing act.

When I round the corner to Shanti's block, she's already sitting on the front steps waiting for me. "How'd I do?" she asks when I come into view. She gestures to her clothes before eyeing the bikes with a triumphant smile. She looks cute today in a simple blue t-shirt and black shorts. Her hair is pulled back in a low ponytail, and she's got her sneakers on.

"You're perfect. I-I mean, *it* is. Your outfit." I drop my gaze from hers and silently curse the flare of warmth on my cheeks. Pulling the bike helmet off one of the handlebars, I hold it out to her.

"I like your outfit, too," Shanti says, and I lift my gaze just as she's trailing hers over me. She pauses on my vest and nods, adding, "Very much."

Ma, you're a frickin' queen!

I quirk a grin, Shanti's compliment reaching all the way to my toes.

"This won't tighten," she mutters, fiddling with the strap on the helmet.

"Can I?" Pointing to her helmet, I wait until Shanti nods before moving in. Her hands fall away, mine replacing the spot under her chin. I could ask her to remove the helmet, but where's the fun in that? Her bike is separating us, but I'm still close enough to hear Shanti's breath quicken. I bite back a smile.

"How don't you have a hundred girlfriends already?" Shanti blurts, her eyes widening as they meet mine.

My lips twitch, but I go back to tightening her helmet and murmur, "I'd be very surprised if there were a hundred queer girls on PEI." I chuckle, backing away when I've finished. "But seriously, I've always been too busy with softball for all that."

Shanti rolls her lips inward, and the action pulls my attention to the rest of her face. The long slope of her nose, the two fine slashes of her dark eyebrows, her perfect oval jawline and chin. Her lips move, "And now?"

I swallow hard, hesitating at the unknowingly loaded question. Am I not as busy as I was pre-Shanti? My goal to make the provincial team and eventually play at the college level hasn't changed. So what *has*?

I shrug. "I met you."

10 *First Base*

WHEN WE REACH Heather Moyse Park, we're both sweating from the summer's heat. Shanti seems happy though, maybe even a bit surprised at my choice of date ideas, and looks around the parking lot. "It's so pretty here."

"Wait 'til we get in farther. It's definitely worth the bike ride."

I slip the backpack off my shoulders, glad to be rid of the extra weight, and take out two bottles of water. "I thought we'd walk around for a bit, then have a picnic. What do you think?" I ask, handing one off to her.

Shanti gratefully accepts the water, uncapping the bottle and taking a few sips before a shy smile breaks through. "I think you might be a bit of a romantic, Rory Taylor."

I bark a laugh, "If I am then I learned from the best."

"Your mom?"

We lock our bikes up and make our way into the park. The weight of my bag feels like it'll tip me backwards.

Probably added too many ice packs.

"My dad," I admit, grateful when my chest doesn't do its usual twist at the mention. My smile is faint. "Definitely. He'd always plan these grand date nights for Ma. Not expensive, 'cause we never had much, but well thought out, ya know? And if they couldn't get a sitter, they'd bring me along."

"That's the sweetest thing ever."

Shanti's shoulder brushes mine as we near the walking trail. Her fingers are casually tickling the back of my hand, so I slip it into hers, interlocking our fingers. "What about your parents? What are they like?"

"Nice," Shanti says slowly. The corner of her mouth tugs up as our eyes meet. "So long as they're not left alone for too long. When I left, Dad was sleeping in the spare bedroom."

I wince, my tongue suddenly thick, and an apology tumbles out. "And here I am basically bragging about mine."

"It's okay, really." Shanti gives my hand a squeeze. "They think I don't know that's why they sent me here for the summer."

"You didn't want to come?" The idea of Shanti digging her heels in to stay home, and therefore us never meeting, doesn't sit well with me.

"Not at first, no. I had an ideal summer job lined up, working at a used bookstore," she shrugs. "My mom made up some excuse about my grandparents needing help, but I know they wanted me gone so my dad could move out. It's long overdue if you ask me."

"You want them divorced?" I couldn't imagine my parents splitting, not even if Dad never got sick. They take the entire "'til death" in their vows seriously.

"I want them happy," Shanti corrects, patient as ever, and I can't help but admire her maturity. I know most people our age wouldn't take their parents splitting nearly as well.

We reach a bridge crossing a swamp, and when Shanti stops to lean against the railing, I follow suit. Silence stretches out for several minutes until a dog barking in the distance breaks Shanti out of her thoughts. She glances up at me, her deep brown gaze sucking me in. "What happened to your dad?"

"Oh. *Oh.*" I swallow, tugging my hand from hers. I start to pace, needing to move, needing distance. Shanti must be a mind reader, because she begins walking along the path again. I follow behind, my long legs easily keeping stride, but her question plagues me like Dad's illness itself. Even though I knew it'd come eventually, I think I hate that question the most.

"I'm sorry, Ror, I didn't mean to pry."

Shanti's gentle use of my nickname is a balm to my misery, and when I look at her again, nothing but kindness glistens behind those gorgeous brown eyes. Eyes the colour of the darkest chestnut yet warmer than a field of sunflowers. I blink, a gush of air leaving me, and I croak, "Pa has ALS. Ever heard of it?"

Shanti shakes her head, and it doesn't surprise me. ALS isn't a well-known disease. I swallow past the lump in my throat, looking down at my feet as we walk. "Basically, it'll shut his muscles down, one at a time, until he becomes a prisoner in his own body." I hesitate at the dampness around my eyes, struggling to continue, "S-started two years ago. He . . . he used to work for a contractor, building houses, ya know? One day, his legs gave out on the roof of a four-storey." *Legs Pa used to run with me.* My vision blurs. "If it hadn't been for the harness, he would've fell. They cramped up twice more before he finally went to the doctor."

"That sounds horrible, Rory, I'm so sorry."

Shanti's hand is back in mine, and I lean in to her comfort. Wiping my eyes, I finish gruffly, "Took months for a diagnosis, but it was fine, you know? Ma got him a wheelchair when he just couldn't hold himself up anymore. We'd still play catch, and he'd wheel himself out of the van to watch my games. And then not even a year later, his hands and arms started going."

"A-and now?"

I grimace, thinking of how spirited my father still is after everything he's lost. "His mind still works, and he's got partial use of his left hand. He can still speak some, but eventually, he'll rely on technology to help when he can't anymore. He already . . . can't say my name right," I choke.

We land at the gazebo, and I guide Shanti in to take a seat. The conversation's shifted now, like an oncoming storm cloud, and I grapple for my earlier excitement. The last thing I want is for our date to be overshadowed by depressing thoughts.

"Thank you for telling me," Shanti's voice is filled with emotion, and when I glance over, I'm surprised to see tears glistening on her long lashes. Instinctively, I reach to wipe them away with the pad of my thumb. Our eyes meet.

"Thanks for listening," I husk, skimming my free hand along her jaw to cup her cheek. We're closer than we've ever been, and my fingers are in just the spot to feel when the pulse in her throat kicks up. She licks her lips, and I helplessly watch the movement.

"C–can I kiss you, Shanti?"

"Depends," she whispers, and her hand not holding mine comes to rest on my shoulder. Her pupils dilate, and I know she wants the kiss as much as I do. "Is it to distract you from your thoughts, or because you genuinely want to kiss me?"

"I've wanted to kiss you since the moment I first saw you."

"Okay," Shanti leans in until we're practically nose to nose. My heart pounds heavily beneath my chest as she breathes. "Kiss me, then."

My tongue darts out to moisten my lips, which have gone as dry as my mouth. Kissing Shanti has been at the forefront of my mind, true, but I don't want to rush into it like I do with everything else. I shrug out of my backpack, shifting to face her on the bench, and reach for her glasses. I remove them carefully, resting them on my bag before returning to Shanti once more. My heart's dropped somewhere in the pit of my stomach, and my hands are slick with sweat, but Shanti either doesn't notice or doesn't care as my palms cup her cheeks.

"You're so pretty," I murmur, kissing her forehead and nose first. Shanti's eyes flutter shut, her usual floral scent enveloping my senses as I place purposeful kisses across both cheekbones.

"Rory . . ."

I could fall in love with this girl, I think absently, finally brushing my lips over hers. Lightly at first and then, when it's Shanti who deepens the contact, I have one last fleeting thought as she pulls me closer.

Shit, I think I already am.

★★★

When we get back to the bed and breakfast, neither of us are ready for our date to end. It was only a couple hours ago that we filled up on ham and cheese paninis, spinach salad, Ma's molasses cookies, and cans of sparkling water, but I invite Shanti to grab ice cream with me.

We walk hand in hand down the street to Holman's, a homemade ice cream parlour that's out of this world delish. It's slightly pricier than other dairy bars, but *absolutely* worth it. "I come here a lot with my parents. Jaya and Sky, too." I say, opening the door for Shanti. "Carlos is probably the only one I *haven't* come here with, but only because he doesn't like ice cream. He's psycho like that."

Shanti giggles, not letting go of my hand as we walk through the packed dining area toward the order counter. "Is that a chai tea flavour?" Shanti asks the server, her nose almost touching the display glass. She looks at me in wonder. "I can't believe I'm only just discovering this place!"

I laugh, marvelling at the way she gets excited over the simplest things. If given the opportunity, I'm positive I'd jump at the chance to make her this happy every day.

Once again, I'm quick to pay — which I think is fair since it was my idea in the first place — and once again, Shanti gently scolds me. It's possible, though, that she secretly thinks it's charming. Maybe a teensy bit?

We sit at one of the many picnic tables in the backyard of the parlour and enjoy our cones. "What?" I say, when I catch Shanti watching me with amusement.

"You literally ate most of the picnic. How are you still so hungry?"

Glancing down at my four scoops, one each of Oreo peanut butter, lemon curd blueberry, salted caramel, and key lime pie, I take another long lick. "I couldn't decide. Besides," I pat my flat stomach and grin, "speedy metabolism."

"Clearly," she pouts, but she's laughing as she

gestures to her one scoop. "This'll go straight to my hips."

"Is that your secret?" I tease, skimming my gaze over her until she blushes. My hand rests on her thigh, and I drop a quick kiss on her lips. "Whatever it is, it's working on me, Shanti."

"Smooth, Taylor." Shanti pulls away, but the smile she's sporting is blinding.

"What did you say your favourite book is?" I ask as I'm walking Shanti to her doorstep later. I plan to check it out when I'm alone in case it comes up in conversation. The surprise on her face is priceless, and before I know it Shanti's running into the B&B. She returns a minute later with a book in her hands. "*Annie on My Mind*," she gushes, handing me the paperback. "You can borrow it if you want." She scrunches her nose in that cute way I love. "Never mind, I forgot you're not much of a reader."

"I'll read it," I quickly say, taking the book from her grasp. I'll *make* myself read *Annie on My Mind*, even if it's solely to impress Shanti.

"You'll read it?" Shanti sounds skeptical, as she should. I've never read a book for pleasure in my life. I force a grin out.

"Uh-huh, promise."

11 *A Different Kind of Game*

"'KAY, ALRIGHT, WE'RE IN," Carlos mutters late Sunday evening, his fingers *tap-tapping* on the game controller.

"Yup," I yawn, unable to stop, and my Minecraft avatar disappears for a second. "Man, I'm literally dead on my feet right now." I just got home about an hour ago after playing off-island this weekend in a tournament. Neallie was busy doing provincial team stuff for the Whitecaps and couldn't pitch for the Hot Sparks, so I finally got the chance to pick up her slack.

We went undefeated the entire weekend! I've been riding high ever since. Coach Dan was so impressed he promised to rotate Neallie and me at games from now on.

I can't wait to see her face tomorrow when she finds out.

"Your coffee not kick in yet?" Carlos arches an eyebrow at me before turning back to the small TV I have sitting on a roll cart in my bedroom. The space is barely sufficient for one teenager, let alone when Carlos visits, but at least I can move the TV around when necessary.

"Guess not," I'm almost certain the brew Mom made me is purposely watered down, but I'd never complain, and she knows it. She's never liked me drinking caffeine, especially past suppertime. I figure coffee is a good compromise to say, energy drinks. Mom caught Carlos with one last year and I legit thought she'd stroke out.

"Well I'm gonna find some resources," Carlos glances over just as I let out another yawn. "Can you manage scouting a location to build on, or am I gonna have to do that too?"

Smirking, I sit up straighter on the floor and give my best friend a one-finger salute. "I got this, Sarge, totally. You can count on me."

"Doubt it," Carlos deadpans when another yawn escapes. He laughs, shaking his head and hitting pause on the game. Leaning back against the foot of my bed, he stares up at my old, gross, popcorn plaster ceiling. "We can just talk for a bit."

"*You* wanna talk? Uh-oh, what'd Pascal do?" I joke. Though I could probably talk for a good hour about Shanti, Carlos was never like that.

"Nothing, you shit." Carlos punches me lightly in the arm, but I feel it through my entire wiry frame and wince.

"Easy on the arms," I groan, rubbing the spot with a glower. "These babies helped win eight games this weekend."

"My bad," Carlos apologizes and raises his hands in a show of peace. He snickers, "Maybe you can finally tell me how you and Shanti became girlfriends so fast. I haven't even got to meet her yet."

I'm not so tired that his comment doesn't make me blush, and memories of my date with Shanti on Thursday come to mind. As I was walking home after our date, I kept replaying every moment of the day with Shanti. Our conversation, how it felt just to share the same space, how intensely she makes me feel. That *kiss* — ohmygod, and *what* a kiss it was. As much as I adore Sky, I wish I could go back in time and never waste my first kiss on her.

"I uh, might've . . . sent her a voice clip, officially asking her to be my girlfriend."

It wasn't the coolest way to ask a girl out, but at the time it felt stupid to call her on the phone and I couldn't wait another second. So I hit her up like some millennial would on Facebook, sent her a voice clip, and thirty seconds later I had my answer.

I roll my eyes at Carlos's laughter and press play on the game again. "See if I tell your punk ass anything else."

"What? It's funny, and such a Rory thing to do," Carlos exclaims, his shoulders shaking as he stifles more laughter. "And she said yes?"

"Of course."

We haven't had much opportunity for texting since Thursday, but I'm assuming Shanti still wants a relationship with me. I gesture to the game with my controller, not so much tired anymore as I am annoyed. "Go get us resources. I'll look for a good spot."

"Copy."

We play for about thirty minutes, with minimal talking, before Carlos unhelpfully points out the one thing I've been avoiding.

"I'm glad for you, Ror, but have you forgotten she'll be gone by September? Or is a summer fling all this is?"

I grind my molars, ignoring his stupid question, ignoring the annoying fact that he's right. Shanti leaving is one scenario I never wanted to consider, even if it's the only one there is.

12 Pitcher Playing Shortstop

MONDAY'S AWAY GAME is a slap to the face.

For some strange reason, I thought Coach would look at me differently after keeping the team's head above water this past weekend. I was wrong.

"Taylor, really come alive at shortstop tonight," Coach Dan instructs as we all huddle around the dugout. He doesn't look up from his clipboard, but he's talking to me like my ass wasn't on fire on the mound just yesterday. Frankly, it pisses me off.

"Shortstop?" I echo, and behind my sunglasses, narrow my gaze on the same bushy mustache I've looked at for four years. What does he know, anyway? He's a frickin' real estate agent who used to play league ball back in the day. If this was in the classroom, I could make his life hell for favouring his daughter, but on the field, the red carpet could roll out for Neallie and my input wouldn't ruffle a damn feather. Not in club softball.

God, I miss playing for Chantel.

"Yeah, shortstop. Unless you need to sit this one out and rest?"

"But you said —" The sharp lurch of my stomach makes my throat tighten, and I glance around at all my teammates. Jaya and Sky are closest to me, watching intently as the scene unfolds. Ava is pulling her hair into a fresh ponytail. Char is chewing a wad of gum and looking bored as all get-out. The rest of the team meets my gaze, but no one speaks up on my behalf. Does anyone care about how the hell I'm treated on this team?

Neallie looks up from her phone with a smirk. "You didn't think you'd be taking over when I'm right here, did you?"

I curl my lip in a snarl, biting out, "I think anyone besides you should pitch." Anger blotches my cheeks, but I don't care. Why did I think, for one minute, that the coach would actually keep a promise? He can't even stand up to his own daughter, let alone do anything nice for me.

"Ror, you can play centre if you want," Sky offers. Her hand is on my arm, momentarily diverting my attention from Neallie.

"Okay, now if that's settled —"

"I don't *want* centre," My skin is tight and uncomfortable as I glower down the dugout at the coach. My sinuses burn, and I swallow hard. "I want to pitch." *You promised*, I silently fume.

"Taylor, you pitched all weekend. It wouldn't be good for you or the team to put you on the mound tonight." Coach Dan frowns like I don't have the right to be upset, but it's always the same on this team and I'm sick of it.

My dad is in the stands today, probably eager to see what I can do. I told him and Mom all about the tournament and how well I pitched, and now the coach is gonna take the chance from me when it counts the most?

"What happened to *anyone* pitching? Ava, you can pitch, right?" Neallie's sharp laughter sends my heartbeat into a frenzy and tears prick my eyelids.

"This is such bullshit," I hiss, tearing my blurred gaze from hers. I grab my glove and stalk out of the dugout. My uneven breaths make it hard to hear anything else, and I fight the urge to wipe my eyes. Unless I lose all sense and start openly weeping on the field, my sunglasses should save me.

As I jog to shortstop I scan the sidelines for my folks, and when I see Dad huddled under a blanket next to the bleachers, my steps falter. A deep longing washes over me as I witness Mom kiss his cheek. Not for the first time, a nagging question tickles the back of my mind.

What does any of this matter?

Softball, Neallie drama, my school grades, even Shanti. My old man is on his last quarter mile, freezing under a sweltering sky, and here I am having a tantrum. I should be with *him*, not on this field, and not having Mom drive two hours just so he can see me play.

"Taylor, let's go!"

I hear the coach, but it's not until Mom spots me coming toward them and waves me off that I pause. I take two more steps, giving up and wiping my eyes, torn between what is right or wrong.

This is all for him, Taylor. For Pa, so keep your head in the game.

I grit my teeth, schooling my composure before turning back to the field. Reminders of why I'm doing this filter my jam-packed thoughts, and as I take up my position, that familiar resolve is back. I square my shoulders, taking deep, slow breaths and glance at my team spread throughout the field.

Dad's gonna be gone before I know it. Getting on the provincial team again, applying for scholarships in the fall, all so he can see I'm going places in life, is and always will be my goal. I don't want to be stuck working dead-end jobs on the island like so many others.

I've gotta see this through.

★★★

It's late when we get home. Dad was asleep by the time we hit Kensington but woke the moment his favourite oldies radio station shut off in the van.

"Nice nap?" I ask, cracking a smile as I help him outside.

"Yes," he breathes, and I imagine him making a snarky comment about catching his beauty sleep. I chuckle, reaching to smooth down the kinks in his thinning salt and pepper hair. "All that sleeping hasn't helped your hair growth yet."

"Ha ha." His eyes twinkle.

"C'mon, you two!"

I help guide Dad's wheelchair up the ramp to where Mom is waiting just inside the front door. "Night, Pa. I love you." But he's already dozing off again. Giving him a kiss on the cheek, my heart is heavy as I let Mom take the reins. My smile wobbles slightly as our eyes meet. "You've got him?"

"Always, darling. You can head up to bed, thank you."

Maybe it's from her years of working as a personal aide, or the fact that Dad is frail and underweight now, but Mom still refuses help with his bedtime routine. Somehow, she gets him out of the chair, either with the use of a lift or brute strength, all by herself. At this point, I'm pretty sure she's a superhero.

In the kitchen, I whip up a snack plate before heading upstairs to my room. My uniform is filthy from the few slides I did during the game, so I toss it all into my hamper and pull on a pair of boxers and a sleeveless top. Showering can happen in the morning. I collapse on the bed with my plate of leftover chicken, berries, and one of Mom's cookies, munching as I scroll through my phone and listen to music. Fleetwood Mac's remastered version of "Dreams" came on the radio when I went across this past weekend with Jaya, and ever since, I've been revisiting their earlier albums. There was so much depth to the band in the earlier days — especially when Lindsey and Stevie joined — from the rasp in Stevie Nicks's voice, to the sweetness of McVie's.

Getting lost in an epic song like "Over My Head" is better than obsessing over how horribly I played tonight. That argument in the dugout seriously screwed up my game.

Not to mention upset the team's vibe.

"Music, remember?" I mutter, squinting at the low battery warning on my phone. A text message from Shanti comes in just as I'm digging out my charger.

Hey, still awake? How was your game?

Her thoughtfulness has me smiling, and after plugging the phone in I reply.

Me: The worst, but thanks for asking.

Shanti: Really? I'm sorry. Can we video call, or is it too late?

The house is silent, so my parents might already be asleep, but there's nothing more I want right now than to see Shanti.

"What happened?" she asks the moment she appears on screen. She's curled up under a thin blanket, her head resting on one arm as she watches me in worry.

A soft sigh leaves me, my body instantly relaxing around her. I fill Shanti in on what's been happening, how I lost my position on the Whitecaps, and how long the Neallie drama has gone on.

"So is shortstop a bad position?" Shanti frowns, and without her glasses on, her big brown eyes seem to pull me in even more. "From what little I've seen, I thought that was where all the action is."

"Shortstop is awesome, and I like to think I'm good at it. But pitching is . . ." I trail off, wondering how I can explain it without sounding immature. Somehow saying, *"Because Neallie stole it from me!"* doesn't sound like it'd go over well. "Standing on the pitcher's mound, everyone cheering you on, everyone waiting on you. It's a powerful feeling."

"So you like having control. That makes a lot of sense, actually."

I frown. I've never considered it being a control issue, but I don't like the idea of it being about attention. "It does?"

Shanti nods, and when the softest smile graces her mouth, it feels like she's wrapped me in a hug through the phone. "Rory, so much of your life right now is out of your control. Losing your spot on the Whitecaps, your dad being sick, how unknown the future is. Pitching gives it back temporarily."

With a slack jaw, I slump against my headboard, shook at Shanti's reasoning. Is she right? Is my desire to pitch stemming from how out of control my life is?

13 Pressure on the Mound

A GUST OF HOT AIR BREEZES through my parted lips as I ready myself for the pitch. The burden of the softball feels foreign to me, like I'm gripping the weight of the world in my hand. The distant hoots and hollers from teammates and fans are often a comfort, but tonight I wish I could drown out the noise with a soothing track from the sixties. Maybe Janis Joplin's "Cry Baby" or Jimi Hendrix's "The Wind Cries Mary."

You can do this. No need for nerves, Taylor.

My mind is everywhere but the game — thinking of Shanti, thinking of my parents. None of them could make it, and a significant piece of me is still in the armchair beside my old man's bed.

Squinting down the line at home, I briefly meet the batter's gaze before shifting to Jaya crouched in her catcher's position. She signals for a curveball, but I shake my head. My pitches so far this game have bordered on embarrassing. I need something slow and easy, preferably unexpected. Jaya makes another signal, almost as if she's read my mind. I take a deep breath and nod.

Sweat trickles down my back, slipping past my boxers as I poise for the pitch. The sensation is ick, mostly because I never notice minor things during a game. My whole body feels strange in my uniform, and as I whip the ball forward, I know straightaway it's a goner.

"Shit, *shit.*"

"BALL!"

I cringe as the ball sails wide toward the backstop behind the batter's box. Jaya scrambles for the ball like a pro but the throw was so wild I doubt even Aubree Munro could catch the damn thing.

"Get it, get it!" Char screams as all hell breaks loose. I watch in momentarily stunned silence as the runner on third with Char takes off for home, before snapping out of it and dashing forward to catch the ball from Jaya if need be. Jaya gets the ball just as the opp is about to cross, and then there's a mad dance around home plate as the opp and Jaya play a vicious game of tag. The girl fakes a left, and Jay stumbles, losing any leverage she had.

"SAFE!"

The metallic taste of blood coats my tongue, and I realize I've been gnawing the inside of my cheek pretty hard. A sudden squeezing sensation around my ribs robs me temporarily of breath, and I swallow several times. My hand goes to my throat, tugging at the uncomfortably tight jersey.

"Rory, hey."

Jaya's in front of me now, and I blink in surprise. How had I not realized a time out was issued?

"Look at me, Ror," Jay demands, taking hold of the front of my pitcher's mask and tugging my face closer. Our eyes meet. "What's wrong?"

What isn't wrong? I want to laugh, cry, feel sorry for myself. My dad was too sick to come to tonight's game, I haven't seen Shanti in days because of our clashing schedules, and now I'm pitching at my worst. *Take your pick.*

My throat tightens, and I tear my gaze from Jay's. "Nothing."

"Well, snap out of it then. We need you here, not out there." Jay points toward the parking lot with the finger not currently tangled in my face mask. Her eyes narrow in that defiant way she has. "Neallie's not here, Ror. Tonight is *your* night. So *take* it."

"Take it," I echo, clearing my throat. "Gotcha, okay."

"Rip it right out from under the Riptides," Jay jokes, holding her fist out for me to bump before tossing the ball to me.

As much as we try, the team doesn't take anything from the Riptides. They win in a humiliating 7–3 finish.

I don't stick around for Jaya and Sky after the game. I'm still raw, and the last thing I want is for them to witness me accidentally coming apart. I trudge home with my skateboard tucked in the straps of my bag, feeling too out of it to do anything more than walk. For once I'm glad my parents couldn't make it. They'd have insisted on an after-game milkshake at Holman's, and watching as Mom feeds Dad, along with consoling me over the game, would have surely broken me.

Except for the lone outdoor light Mom must have left on for me, the house is dark when I get home. I sneak in as quietly as possible, setting my bag under the bench in the hallway like I always do. Fatigue has me bypassing the kitchen, and I head straight upstairs long enough to grab my PJs and towel for a shower.

The hot water is a relief to my sore muscles, but all the scrubbing in the world couldn't erase the shame of the last few hours.

Deep, unspent emotion clogs my throat. I close my eyes and let the tears come, hoping that, if nothing else, some of the hurt washes away with the suds and dirt.

I'm much calmer as I make my way into my room a long time later. I drop onto my unmade bed, snatching my cell from the nightstand as I go. A flurry of text messages from Shanti makes me smile for the first time all day. She must have found some downtime after all.

Shanti: Sorry I missed your game. Hope it went well!

I feel bad I've been so busy at work to see you. Miss you, Ror! Xoxo

Shanti: Have you had a chance to read any of the book yet?

Shanti: Are you okay? Jay said you were down tonight. Call me?

Shanti: I'm falling asleep but call me when you get this.

I huff, shaking my head at Shanti's last message sent an hour ago. Surely she doesn't think I'm the type to selfishly keep her up all night?

My gaze lands on the book peeking out from under a pair of surf shorts that never made it into the hamper. I'd forgotten all about my task of reading *Annie on My Mind* to impress the sweet, intelligent, and shy girl I like. Which is pathetic, considering I had all week to start it since I couldn't see Shanti.

I exchange my cell for the book, getting comfortable in bed before opening up to the first page. I expect to feel *meh* at best, downright bored at worst, but instead, I'm sucked into Liza's world with the very first line.

14 Double Play

I'M DEAD TO THE WORLD when Mom shakes me awake.

"Ma, I'm up, stop," I mumble, cracking a bleary eye open to look up at her. The sun flooding my room nearly blinds me, and I groan, "What time is it?"

"Past eight." Mom hovers over my bed, hands on hips. "You feeling okay? You never sleep in."

"Yeah, 'course." Rubbing the sleep from my face, I slowly pull myself to a sitting position. The book tangled in my sheets brings back the night before, and

I realize I must have fallen asleep reading *Annie on My Mind.*

That's two nights in a row.

"What are your plans for the day?"

"I dunno." I swallow. "How's Pa?"

Mom's smile is soft, considering. "Good, no doubt wanting you to live your life and stop worrying about him."

I run my fingers through my hair, and a strained chuckle escapes. "Impossible."

Mom heads for the door, calling over her shoulder, "Breakfast is keeping warm in the oven when you're ready."

"Thanks, Ma."

When she leaves, I hurry to get dressed. I've already got a text from Sky and Jaya, wondering if I can hang today, but all I can think about is seeing Dad with my own eyes to make sure he's okay.

"Good morning," I say when I walk into the kitchen.

"Morning, Rory," Dad's automated voice rings out in the kitchen. He's pulled up to the table in his wheelchair, with the Eyegaze machine close by. There's a hint of a smile there when I drop a kiss on his cheek.

"You sound amazing on that, Pa," I say, and continue on to the stove.

"Thanks, I have . . ." Dad trails off, taking several moments before the rest of his sentence comes out, "been practising."

I laugh, "You have! You'll be singing in no time. Did you eat yet?"

"Yes."

I sit beside him with my omelet and porridge, watching as he navigates the internet on the display screen using just his eyes. He looks pretty good today, just like Mom said, and it makes me breathe a little easier. I hate leaving the house when he's having a bad day.

I spend the next hour with Dad, talking and reading the paper while Mom slips out to run errands. By the time she's back, I've made up my mind to surprise Shanti today. We've been missing each other all week, and she's been busy helping her grandparents. From what I understand, they could use an extra set of hands. That's where I'll come in.

★★★

I'm not sure of the protocol when arriving at a bed and breakfast, so I ring the doorbell instead of just walking in. My hands are clammy, and when an older man comes to the door, I'm aggressively wiping them on my jeans.

"Can I help you?"

"Hi, yes, I'm Rory Taylor." Stopping mid-wipe, I thrust my hand out for him to take, and the smile on my face quivers. I've never shown up on a girlfriend's doorstep before. "I'm, um, friends with Shanti. You must be Mr. Devi."

"Why, because I'm Indian?" His bushy eyebrows narrow, and I swallow hard. Had I somehow offended him?

"No, sir, b-because you answered the door. Is this . . . not your B&B?"

A booming laugh tumbles out of the small man, way louder than I'd have expected, and I jump a little. He claps me on the back, gathering me into an awkward side hug where the top of his head rests just below my chin. "I like you, Rory Taylor. Come, come inside."

"I know all about your friendship with my granddaughter," Mr. Devi rambles as he guides me through the quaint historic home. "You're all she talks about."

Warmth floods my chest as I follow him up to the second floor. I bite back a smile. "I'm glad we met, sir."

I spot Shanti leaving one of the rooms, a bag of garbage in her hands, but she drops it the moment she sees us. "Rory!" Her half-muted squeal fills the hallway, and I can't help but laugh as she takes off toward me. I catch her in my arms, my eyes drifting closed of their own accord, and sigh, about to bury my face in the crook of her neck when she abruptly pushes me away. "What are you doing here?"

"Thought I'd see if you or your grandparents needed help today." A sheepish smile appears, and I dart a glance at Mr. Devi before whispering, "And I missed you."

"Ditto," Shanti gushes, and not even a foot from her grandfather, she grabs my face in her hands and plants me one right on the mouth.

"Interesting friendship you two have, Rory Taylor," Mr. Devi says, his brown eyes full of mischief.

I blush, not knowing what to say to that.

I work all weekend with the Devis, mostly helping Mr. Devi with maintenance around the B&B. I like working with my hands, and after watching Dad build stuff over the years, I learned a thing or two. In between backyard deck repairs on Saturday, Mrs. Devi feeds me any chance she gets. Come Sunday afternoon, I've fallen in love with both Indian food and Shanti's grandparents. I can't believe that after all these years of knowing Jaya, I've never actually met them.

"How are things going?"

I glance up to where Shanti is placing a tray of goodies on a nearby table, watching as she pours two glasses of iced tea. She hands me one, along with two cookies.

Setting the paintbrush down, I gratefully accept, "Thanks." I smile, scooting closer to the edge of the deck.

Shanti looks past me to the freshly restored deck, nodding in approval. "Thank *you*. I can't believe you just showed up!"

"Mhmm. It's been nice to get out of my head for a while."

Shanti sits beside me, leaning in to kiss my cheek before lacing her fingers in mine. "Wanna talk about it?"

Shaking my head, I smile a little. "No."

Rehashing Thursday night's game, or how sick my dad is won't help anything, and besides, Shanti already knows all that. I'm the one still obsessing over things.

That evening, when the projects are finished,

Shanti and I sneak away to the hammock in the backyard. It's the first time all weekend we've been truly alone, and it's the perfect ending to a great two days. Being around her, and getting to know her grandparents, has made me fall even harder.

"What about this song?" I ask, sliding the lyric page up in the Spotify app. We're cuddled up in the hammock, sharing my AirPods and listening to my classic sixties playlist. So far, my love of oldies isn't something we have in common, but I can respect that.

"The beat is good, but sounds like there's a lot of mistrust going on. Elvis, right?" Shanti tilts her face up to mine, accepting the gentle kiss I drop to her lips.

"Yeah," I chuckle, "one of my favourite songs, too. You wound me, Shanti."

"Aww, poor baby," she jokes, and playfully swats my arm before going in for another kiss. We linger there, our foreheads pressed together and our noses touching. "It'll be interesting to know what you think of the music I like."

"Let's find out." An easy enough solution, and I

pull away enough to access my phone once more. I hand it to her. "Hit me with it."

Shanti hesitantly grips the phone. "Oh, I dunno. I'm very much a mood listener, I . . . some of it might be stupid."

"Try me."

Shanti bites her lip. "Okay."

I watch as she types the title of a song into the search bar, laughing outright when an electric guitar, followed by heavy drums, fills my head. "Is this the mood you're in right now?"

Shanti laughs too, blushing hard as she fiddles with my phone again. "No, but the World Alive is one of my favourite bands. This is more my mood right now."

A moment later the soft intro of piano keys begins, and I catch my breath as the country singer's gravelly voice belts out heartbreaking lyrics. "Damn."

"Tyler Childers," Shanti softly explains. "The song is about losing his love too early."

I look at the screen for the song title and read "In

Your Love," sighing as we continue listening. Does this mean Shanti's upset, or just in a pensive mood? I hold her tighter against me, deciding a subject change is in order. My lips graze her forehead. "What are the steps in getting your book published?"

"Ugh, *so* many, and all very overwhelming. I've never let anyone read it, ever," Shanti admits, glancing at me sheepishly.

"Not even Jaya?"

She shakes her head, a low blush deepening the dusty shade of her skin. "What if it sucks?"

"Sucks?" My eyebrows lift in surprise. I reach for a strand of Shanti's hair, twirling it around my finger, "Babe, your book sounds amazing."

A smile blossoms, and then those brown eyes twinkle. "'Babe'?"

I grin, sweeping my arms around her and kissing her deeply. When we come up for air, we cuddle into each other once more. "We should do this every weekend."

I wish, I think, but say quietly, "The Eastern

Qualifiers are next weekend." It's a tournament being held in New Brunswick this year, where all the teams hoping to play at the end-of-summer championship compete. In the end, only a handful of teams will continue on, usually a team or two from each of the eastern provinces.

"Right, I forgot," Shanti sounds wistful, but when she presses play on the sad song from before, I wonder if we're thinking the same thing.

August is fast approaching, and in September she'll be flying home.

15 Opposition

THE FOLLOWING WEEK is jam-packed with work, practice, and spending as much time as possible with my folks and Shanti. I hitch a ride with Jaya to the Eastern Qualifiers tournament, where our team MAKES IT IN!! And that's without Neallie's help, since she was playing a tournament in Maine at the same time with the rest of the provincial team. My pitching game was on point, and in my opinion, the Hot Sparks play way better without Neallie.

On the last day of July, Jaya's dad drives us to our game in Kensington. Shanti tags along. Jay teases us, claiming that Shanti only comes to all these games because of me, but it doesn't bother me . . . at least not until after the game. We join the team and parents at Pizza Delight for a celebratory dinner after our win, and when Shanti sits beside me, the whispers start.

"What's *she* doing here? I don't have my boyfriend hanging off my arm every game," Neallie hisses from the other end of the long, rectangular table, and not nearly as quietly as she likely thinks she is.

"Can you say 'groupie'?" Kamryn giggles between her and Becky, who smirks.

I scowl, aware of the pulse pounding in my throat. I open my mouth, fully prepared to defend Shanti, but Jaya beats me to it.

"Shanti's my cousin. *Family*," Jaya declares, jutting her chin out as if daring the girls to continue. "She'll be wherever I want her to be, got it?"

That seems to shut them up, but their comments leave a lot to unpack, and it stays with me for hours after. I hate how I get so hung up on things, stuff others let slide or forget all about. Most of all, I hate how Neallie and her friends might be right. For so long I've been solely focused on softball and being there for my dad. Since meeting Shanti, I'm the only player bringing their significant other around any chance she gets.

On Tuesday, the first day of August — which also happens to be a softball practice evening — I take Shanti to a local author reading at the library. I hate that I'm missing practice, but Shanti loves books and I figured it would be the perfect date. The reality is that my need to make her happy trumps almost everything else these days.

"I'm usually not into sports, but I love watching you and Jaya play. You're really good, Ror," Shanti admits as we're walking back to the B&B hand in hand.

I'd fully planned to talk to her about maybe hanging back from games, but hearing her excitement not only stopped that train of thought, it completely derailed it off the tracks. I've missed having someone cheer me on like that. My parents come to the games when they can, and have always supported me, but nothing has been the same since Dad's diagnosis.

"You look hot in uniform," Shanti adds with a wink, before looking away and taking a concentrated lick of the cone we stopped at Holman's for.

Flushing, I quickly change the subject. "I've been looking at universities," I begin, although that's kind of a lie. There is only one university I'm interested in, and it just so happens to be in the same general area where Shanti lives. I clear my throat. "I'm gonna ask Jay to record me playing, so I can send recruitment videos to the coaches."

"Hey, that's great news!" Shanti exclaims, nudging me in the arm. She takes in my grave expression, her smile falling a little. "Isn't it?"

"Mhmm." I nod, and it's my turn to pretend the ice cream I'm holding is something top secret I've been charged with investigating. No matter what I do, every single decision I've made in the last few years has been with my father in mind. I've sacrificed *so much* for him to see me succeed. How am I only now realizing it means I'll need to leave him in order to do it? I'll be across the country, and he'll just be here . . .

Dying.

My stomach drops, and I pitch forward on the sidewalk. My mouth waters like I'm gonna hurl.

"Ror?" Shanti's hand is on me, squeezing my shoulder. "Talk to me, babe."

Tears blur my vision, and I shake my head. "Oh, God." I choke, dropping my cone to bury my face in my hands. My shoulders shake as I sob, but Shanti ditches her ice cream and crouches with me on the sidewalk, wrapping her arms around me in a tight hug.

"How c-can I leave him?" The question comes out rushed and blubbering, and at first, I'm not sure Shanti can make anything out. My hand slips down to rub the ache in my chest, and it's so deep inside it feels like my heart is splitting apart.

"It'll be okay, Rory. It'll be okay," Shanti murmurs, rubbing comforting circles across my back.

My sobbing drowns her out, so eventually, she says nothing at all and just holds me.

Tension rises the moment I step onto the field for our home game on Wednesday. Conversations teeter off, and as I set my bag down inside the dugout, the silence is so loud you could hear a pin drop. Frowning, I try to shrug it off, bending to tuck my skateboard in under the bench.

Sky plops down beside me, never one to keep an elephant in a room for long, and hisses, "You missed practice for a *date*?"

I dart her a glance, immediately stilted at the annoyance rolling off her and huff out, "So what? People miss practice all the time. It's not like the Hot Sparks is a provincial team."

The moment the words are out I wish I could reel them in again. I turn back to my bag and yank the zipper down. It's unlike me to go off on Sky, but I haven't been quite right since my breakdown the night before. Unloading on Shanti might have brought the two of us closer, but that's about the only good thing to come from it. I've been super emotional and tired all day.

"Yeah, but you never miss a practice." Sky stares up at me in confusion.

"I'm sorry, okay? Can we just pretend I'm human for a minute?" I demand, snatching my jersey from the bag and putting it on.

Coach Dan interrupts our stare down to give the pre-game talk, and ten minutes later I'm jogging onto the field to shortstop. Twenty minutes after that, the team's frustration with me becomes noticeable.

The ball is hit deep out into left field, but when I act as a cutoff, Sky completely ignores me and throws the ball toward first. "What the hell? I was here for it!" I shout, slapping my hands against my thighs before running back to shortstop. Kamyrn catches the ball too late and I kick the ground. The opp on third races home at the same time, already scoring their second run.

I pull Sky aside when we finally run off the field. "Be pissed all you want, but don't take it out on the game."

"Thought you said club teams don't matter?" Sky smirks.

The entire game is like this. Everyone on the team seems to have something to say about my missed practice, and our game suffers for it. What galls me the most is the look of pure satisfaction on Neallie's face that everyone is on the outs with me.

16 No Hitter

"SO, THINKING OF YOUR TOP TEN BIRTHDAYS, how's this one ranking?" I ask Shanti a week later. We're waiting outside a restaurant near the wharf in Montague, having spent the day playing tourist on the eastern end of the island. It's been a treat for me too, since it's been years since I came down for something besides softball.

I glance at my phone, probably for the fifth time, but I can't help it. Carlos and Pascal are taking forever in the restaurant, and I can't be late for my game in Charlottetown.

"Epic, since I'm spending it with you."

Shanti's response is the cheesiest ever, and I laugh, tucking my phone away and tugging her into me for a kiss. "You sap," I gush against her lips.

She giggles, pulling me closer still until there's not an inch of space separating us. Her palm cups my face, her eyes studying mine. And then she says, "I'm gonna apply to Simon Fraser too."

"You are?" My eyes widen in disbelief. "For real?"

Shanti laughs as a huge grin transforms her face. "Of course! Like I'd give you up so easily."

"I'm so excited!" I squeal, wrapping my arms around her waist and lifting her up to twirl her around.

Shanti breaks into more giggles, half-heartedly pushing at my shoulders, "Stop, you're gonna break your back!"

"No way."

Her gaze collides with mine, still dancing with laughter, and the beauty of it catches my breath. Slowly, her smile fades until it's just her shoulders left trembling. We stare at each other, soaking the other in. I'm the happiest I've been in a long time, and I figure, if I have to leave the island, there's no one I'd rather go to than Shanti. She is . . . she brings so much good to my life. I don't ever want it to end.

I reach out and trace the bridge of her nose with my finger, then her lips, not caring if anyone walking past has a problem. "Shanti, I think I lo —"

"Okaaayy, let's bounce, Ror," Carlos shouts, breaking me out of Shanti's spell. I pull away from her, surprised to find my friend already in the driver's seat.

I rub the back of my neck sheepishly. "We better go," I mutter to Shanti, and as we race to the car, my heart is in my throat. *What* was I about to say?

I take Shanti's hand in the backseat, my thoughts whirling around. *Do I love her?* I've never felt this way for anyone before.

"Ah damn," Carlos grumbles, smacking the steering wheel. The car sputters as he slowly pulls onto the shoulder of the highway.

I perk up in my seat. "What?"

He drops a few more choice curse words before the car shuts off completely. "We're out of gas."

"What?" Shanti's mouth falls open, and the gravity of the situation kicks in.

"Are you serious right now? Carlos, we're already gonna be late!" I whine, checking my phone for the tenth time.

Carlos meets my worried gaze in the rearview mirror and grimaces, "Sorry, bro."

★★★

We pull up to the West Royalty field almost two hours later. I sprint from the car the second Carlos parks, dragging my duffel bag behind me. While we were waiting for roadside assistance I changed into my uniform pants, but I'm awkwardly pulling my jersey on over my sleeveless top as I head for the dugout.

Coach Dan hardly spares me a glance when I go by. There are only a few players left in the dugout, as most are on the field. I grab my glove. "What's the inning?" I ask the quiet girl, Molly.

A low voice comes from behind. "The game's half over, Taylor."

My shoulders stiffen at the annoyance in the coach's voice. I catch his scowl when I turn around, "I'm sorry, Coach. We ran out of gas, and —"

He holds up a hand, "Save it. You're sitting this one out."

"You're benching me?" My mouth gapes open.

"Hell, Taylor, you're benching yourself."

"This is bullshit," I growl, slamming my glove down on top of my bag.

It only gets worse when my team comes back from the infield. Neallie saunters into the dugout with a shit-eating grin, purposely plopping down beside me.

"What?" I snap, slouching further in my seat.

Becky and Kamyrn sit around us. My jaw begins to tick, my temper crackling.

"I don't get you, Taylor." Neallie folds her arms across her chest. "You used to be a challenge. Not as good as me, but a close second. Now you're letting some girl ruin all your chances of getting back on the provincial team. You know, the team that *actually* matters."

"Not to mention being a shitty teammate," Becky throws in, staring down her nose at me.

"It wasn't Shanti's fault I was late," I grit out, clenching my fists at my sides.

"Yeah well, the team sees you slacking. Even Jaya," Kamryn tells me, snapping her fingers rudely in my face. "Wake up, Rory."

"Piss off," I grumble, standing up to get away from them. I move to where Jay and Sky are picking up their bats, but when they see me they shake their heads and turn away.

"You've gotta be kidding me."

17 Pre-Game Talk

I HIT THE SNOOZE BUTTON THREE TIMES before finally tossing the covers aside. My head's pounding, and for several minutes I just lie there and stare up at the ceiling. There's a pressure in my chest that's been there for the better part of two days, and ignoring Shanti's messages yesterday only deepened the feeling. Guilt gnaws at me for pushing her away, but having the entire team turn their backs on me is the wake-up call I needed.

"What am I doing?" I groan, rubbing a hand over my face. My tired eyes are puffy and blurry, proof of how committed I was to getting as little sleep as possible. I must've tossed and turned for half the night before finally crashing.

My feet land on the soft rug in front of my bed, and my gaze drifts to my phone on the nightstand. I reach for it on instinct before freezing, my hand hanging in limbo in the air. Shanti sent several messages yesterday and last night, and I can't deal with that right now. Can't deal with her hurt or confusion for me ghosting her, but then again, I could always claim I was too busy or tired for a conversation.

Except for the fact you left her on read.

I cringe. Girls *hate* that. Or at least that's the impression I've gotten from Carlos, whenever he checks messages from Pascal and forgets to reply.

"Ugh. I can't with all the drama lately," I mutter, leaving my phone resting on the nightstand. I head to the bathroom instead to wash up for work. I slept in, so there's zero chance of running this morning. I stop just outside the den on the way to the kitchen, listening for movement beyond the door. Mom is speaking in hushed tones, nothing I can make out, but I'm guessing Dad's awake. Knocking softly, I wait for the okay before pushing the door open.

"Morning." A small smile forms at the sight of the two of them. Dad's in his wheelchair with a towel around his shoulders, and Mom is shaving his face. After each stroke of the razor, she rinses it out in a bowl of water on a wheeled table.

"Hey, love. You just getting up?" Mom asks, pausing long enough to glance up at me.

I nod, coming more into the room to give them both a kiss. "Pa, you're looking spiffy this morning." His eyes twinkle with affection, and I give him a one-armed squeeze around his shoulders.

"Unless something changes, we plan to make it to your game tonight. It's in Summerside, right?"

"Uh-huh." My shoulders droop a little when the tension within the team comes to mind. Will my parents be able to tell something's off?

All because I met Shanti.

For the first time ever, I hope my parents can't make it.

★★★

I arrive early to our final game before the championships, needing to chalk the lines and clean up the bases on this field and the one beside us. It's a tedious part of my summer job, but I can listen to music and it helps take my mind off things. The canteen staff are setting up when I'm finishing the last bit around the batter's box, and they wave to me when I bring the field chalker to the shed.

I change into my uniform, still the first player there, but that suits me just fine. I'm in a solitary mood anyway. Once my gear is on, I do a walkabout around the field, all the times I've played here flooding my memories.

Fourteen years and I finally get benched.

It hurts to think about.

My phone vibrates in my back pocket, and I

swallow when I see the recent messages from Shanti on my lock screen. I'm a piece of shit for not responding to any of them, but I don't know what to say that won't make things worse or fill me with even more doubt. I'm a coward. Maybe I was naive for thinking I could have it all.

Off the Wall by Michael Jackson starts playing, and the instrumental intro to the album is just white noise in my head as I find myself approaching the pitcher's mound. I step into position and wish we were playing a late game tonight. Then the stadium lights would light up the field and set the mood. I can already see it playing out in my mind.

Fans are on the edge of their seats, some screaming my name, some screaming the opposition's. My parents are there too, my dad excitedly pumping his arms in the air. I turn in a slow circle, spotting my teammates in the outfield, poised for the moment the batter makes contact . . .

"Hey, Ror! Think fast."

I blink, spotting Jay hovering over home plate and a ball soaring toward me. My gloved hand shoots up seconds before the ball hits me in the face. In catching the ball, my footing is lost and I stagger back, popping one of my earbuds out. "What the hell, Jay?"

"Wanna practice for a bit, or are you gonna just stand there daydreaming?"

"Oh, you're talking to me now?" I glower, hoping she can see how annoyed I am. I arch my leg forward and whip the ball down the line. She catches it easily.

"Why are you ignoring Shanti?"

"I'm not," I lie, before receiving another harder-than-necessary throw. Another ball aimed at my head. She must be as pissed off as I am.

"Bull, Ror. I don't know what's gotten into you, but you're acting like an idiot." Instead of throwing the ball once more, she drops it on the ground and heads to the dugout.

Great, another night of this shit. Grinding my molars, I head off the field as well. Spectators are slowly arriving, and most of the Hot Sparks are in the dugout. I take a seat in my usual spot, sipping water as Coach Dan gathers everyone around.

Sky nudges me, holding out her bag of sunflower seeds. "Want some?"

I shrug, recognizing the peace offering. "Sure, thanks." The coach starts his pre-game talk, so we don't say anything else, but it's nice knowing at least Sky is still team Rory.

"It's the last game before the championships and I want everyone giving their best out there tonight." Coach Dan glances around the dugout, his gaze landing on mine for a second longer than everyone else's. I stare him down, refusing to look away. He sighs. "Taylor, you're on the mound this game."

My jaw drops in disbelief.

"*What?*" Neallie snaps, jumping to her feet. "Coach —"

"— At least for the first few innings," Coach Dan continues, speaking over his daughter. His *furious* daughter, if her reddened cheeks are any indication.

"Thank you, Coach." I keep a straight face, but inside I'm jumping up and down. This will be the first game all season my parents see me pitch. *If they even come.*

"This is totally unfair! Rory goes from getting benched to stealing *my* position?"

Dayum. If Neallie could shoot lasers from her eyes, then right now I'd be a crispy pile at her feet. I smirk, grabbing my glove from the bench and drawling out, "No need to be salty, superstar."

Neallie growls, stomping out of the dugout, and I can't help but laugh. Coach Dan grabs my arm, his expression a bit too grave for my mood right now. "Don't let me down, Taylor."

I shove down the incessant worry over my parents watching me play, or whether Shanti came to the game, and puff out my chest a little.

"Not a chance, sir."

18 *Time Out*

"Pitcher, pitcher, what's wit' ya? You're gonna strike, strike, strike 'em dead is ya?"

The mounting cheers bring a smile forth, and I reach to wipe the trail of sweat running down my face. I'm feeling good. Tonight is *good*. I'm playing like I used to, totally in the zone. It's the top of the fourth, and it seems like the entire team is pulling their weight, all working together.

The announcer calls out the newest batter walking up to the plate. I immediately recognize Mandy from previous games, and with Char and Becky moving backwards from the bases, they must as well. She's often a hard hitter, and with only one runner on second, she currently has nothing to lose.

Licking my dry lips, I narrow my eyes, focusing on Mandy's stance and the way her left arm tucks tightly into her ribs. With the way she's positioned, she could totally be going for a bunt. It's not her usual style, but maybe she's noticed my teammates moving back as well. It's a good strategy, one I've done myself.

Jaya signals for a curveball, and I shake my head. Only a drop or rise pitch will ensure my opp swings and misses or fouls. If I'm wrong, I risk Mandy hitting a home run, but I don't think I am.

When Jay and I come to a silent agreement, I line my fingers up properly in the ball's stitching, wind my arm up, and make the pitch. My left leg lurches forward as the ball leaves my fingertips, and sure enough, as it closes in on home plate, Mandy makes a delayed attempt to swing at the rising ball.

"STRIKE!"

I roll my shoulders a few times, waiting for Jay to throw the ball back. Instead, she calls a time out and jogs over to me. I squint down at her through my mask. "What?"

Jaya presses the ball into my chest. "Dude, you *know* what. Don't ignore her all game, okay?"

I frown, the not-so-subtle mention of Shanti darkening my mood and stealing my focus long enough that my traitorous gaze immediately tracks her across the field. She's sitting between my parents and Jaya's, and a week ago it would have made me the happiest gay in the world. Now the sight just makes me feel worse. How can I be with Shanti when it gets in the way of softball? I can barely keep up with school and sports, let alone entertain the idea of dating Shanti long distance. No. Neallie was right. I've sidelined my ambitions, and it can't continue.

"The game comes first, *remember?*" I hiss, shoving Jaya away before I do something regrettable, like punch her for real. "Get back behind the plate, Jay."

There's a sour, almost achy feeling beginning in my chest as Jaya runs back to position, and I absently massage the area. My throat burns, and when tears threaten, I wish I had hit her.

Stupid Jaya.

"Good game, good game," I mutter, shaking hands with the other team as I make my way down the line. We won by seven, but it was no thanks to me in the end. After Jaya's mid-game tête-à-tête, I couldn't get my head back in the zone. When Neallie was put in during the top of the fifth, I was *grateful* for the reprieve. Having all those eyes on me when I was so messed up didn't do any good, so Coach heard no complaints from me as I slunk into shortstop for the remainder of the game.

Jaya on the other hand, well, at some point in the

near future, she and I would have *words*. Sabotaging little bitch that she was.

The moment the teams break apart, I escape to the dugout for my belongings. I'm stuffing my glove and water bottle into my bag when someone clears their throat behind me.

"Rory, hi."

My whole body goes rigid at the sound of her soft voice, my posture stiff like granite. Despite the commotion around us, in and out of the dugout, the quickening of my pulse in my ears is loud and uncomfortable. I can feel her behind me, close enough to touch, but I don't turn around. I can't.

God, my legs are quaking.

"Am I not even worth the time it takes to break up with?"

My head hangs at the obvious tremble of her words. My eyelids are wet, and it takes a few times to swallow past the lump in my throat. "Shanti . . ." my voice cracks, and I try again, "I don't want to."

Her palms are against my ribs now, and she

leans into me, her breasts pressing into my back. The warmth of her breath fans my cheek. "Then don't. *Please*, Rory."

I'm shaking. Each bone and tissue now feels like it could collapse in on itself. Tears stream down my cheeks and collect on the curve of my chin. I swipe them away before placing my hand on one of Shanti's. I give her a gentle squeeze, untangling from her embrace.

Slinging my bag over my shoulder, I can't bear to look at her as I choke out, "I'm sorry but, being with you . . . is a distraction I can't afford."

19 *Foul Ball*

"I'M SUPPOSED TO DRIVE to the airport tonight with Jay, but she's been ghosting me since I broke up with Shanti last week. How's that fair?" I arch a questioning brow at Carlos before pushing off the outdoor deck of the quarter pipe with my skateboard. A lukewarm August breeze fans my hot cheeks as I gain speed for my next rail grind, followed by a simple ollie and lazy cruise. I'm careful not to do anything too risky while softball is most important.

You proved that, didn't you, Taylor?

The reminder of Shanti's sobs makes me lose temporary control, and as my board scores off the grind box, I have to jump off before crashing.

Carlos lands nearby on his board, glancing to where mine has rolled into the centre of the bowl. "You good?"

"Bro," I snicker, trying unsuccessfully to shake off the hurt of the last few days. "*Yaas.* 'Course, I'm good."

"No cap? 'Cause I'm having a hard time believing you wanted to end things with Shanti. She's perfect for you, bro. Smart, pretty . . ." Carlos chuckles, shaking his head appreciatively, "I know you're a sucker for curves, and that girl is *thicc*!"

Even though he's paying Shanti a compliment, I give him a shove. "I said I'm *good*. Keep talkin' like a jackass and I'm gonna knee your junk, Carlos."

I stomp over to my runaway skateboard, ignoring the grating laughter behind me. It doesn't help that he's right. Shanti *was* perfect for me. I pushed her away so I could focus on my original endgame, but the reality is harder to stomach. At some point during the fleeting time we've known each other, Shanti captured a vital part of me.

Kind of hard to focus on *anything* when you're missing a piece of your heart.

20 Back to First

I DIG MY CLEATS INTO THE EARTH beside home plate
and brace for impact. The Peterborough pitcher winds
up for the ball's send-off, and, for a fleeting moment,
my eyes close as I take a deep breath.

They fly open and my knees bend seconds before
I swing.

CRACK!!

The alloy smashing against the cork in the softball
is the only thing I hear before I drop my bat and take

off down the line. Elated shouts and rattling of the dugout fence encourage me to pick up the pace, and I breeze past first base and onto second.

"Go back, Taylor, back to first!"

Coach Dan is loud from the sidelines, and the second I pivot I just miss the second base player's tag attempt. As miserable as I am off-field, the excitement of the game has me laughing, and from there, it's a race back to first base. The ball soars past my head, and to my surprise, past the reaching girl on first.

"Shit!" she chirps, taking off after it. The ball only lands a few feet away, and so I spring into a forward slide into the bag, sputtering as dust and pebbles fly into my face at the effort.

"SAFE!"

I laugh again, jumping up to dust myself off. My opp jogs back to me and just shakes her head as I remove my helmet long enough to swipe the sweat off my forehead. The corners of her lips twitch, like she's trying not to smile. "I see you're still a goof on the field, Taylor."

Nudging her hip with mine and getting ready to run again, I spot Kamryn laying into a bunt at-bat before I toss my old-time rival a grin. "I try, Thompson. Good seeing you."

"You, too," she calls out, and I take off again. I'm just about to second base when Kamryn gets out, and I slow to a walk toward the dugout.

The familiar face of Thompson races past me, turning to throw her hands up in a "what can you do?" motion, before flashing a grin and disappearing to her side of the field.

"That's three out for the Hot Sparks, folks," the announcer chimes in from the speaker's box. I vaguely listen to him as I reach my place and snatch up my Gatorade bottle. "We're entering the top of the sixth inning between the Summerside Hot Sparks and this weekend's hosts, the Peterborough Wildcats, and I've gotta say, so far the teams have been neck to neck out there."

"Taylor, you good to continue pitching?"

Nodding, I swallow my mouthful, "Yeah Coach, why?"

Since Neallie plays on the provincial team, she's only permitted to play in one championship, so she didn't come with us to Ontario. Last I heard she and the Whitecaps were playing in the States somewhere.

I used to thrive on the pressure of pitching well, and it was no surprise I'd fought Neallie tooth and nail to be here, but being so far apart from my parents — and Shanti — this weekend's expectations of me might feel too high. Especially since it came with a price.

"You're distracted out there. We need your head in the game, okay?" Coach Dan pats my shoulder, something that surprises us both it seems, since his eyes widen slightly.

An awkward cough leaves me, and I duck my head to move around him before murmuring, "Understood, sir."

★★★

"Hey, Ma," I murmur via video chat hours later, watching as she gets up from my dad's bedside and silently leaves the den. "How's he doing?"

"Your pa is fine, love," Mom whispers, closing the door behind her. As soon as she's in the kitchen she says in a normal voice, "He's strong and resilient and wishes you'd not worry so much."

This makes me chuckle, but talking about Pa like he's just come down with the flu and will recover has my chest aching. *Oh, the lies we tell ourselves.* I clear my throat, picking absently at the loose thread on the hotel bed's comforter. Someone should really have this fixed before the entire blanket unravels.

"How was your first day? Are you in bed already? You could have called in the morning if you were too tired, love."

"I wanted to see him. And you." Shit, this is getting too emotional. I can feel pinpricks of tears threatening. I puff up one of the pillows around me and burrow under the covers more, trying to get comfortable but also distract myself.

"Is Jaya there?"

"No, just me right now."

Jaya was supposed to be rooming with me on our

trip, but with everything that's gone on, I'm not sure she still will. She was here long enough to change out of her uniform after our two games, one of which we lost against New Brunswick.

We talk for a few minutes more, but I mostly wanted to check in on Dad. Although his condition is steadily declining, some days are worse than others. Those are the moments it's hardest to leave his side.

An hour later the emotive lyrics of Carole King's "So Far Away" fill my ears. My thoughts have long shifted back to Shanti, and I've tortured myself by rereading every text message we ever sent, including the last few she sent after we broke up. She'd still been hopeful I'd change my mind, but I couldn't get out of my own way long enough to respond.

The corner of *Annie on My Mind* peeks out from under one of my pillows, a reminder I still have two chapters left in my commitment. There's so much to love about the story, but there's also a certain amount of frustration I feel for the characters. The book was written in a time when the majority of people kept their Bibles close and considered homosexuality a disease. Though I know that level of ignorance and hatred still exists, I'm grateful I've never had to hide my interest in girls.

Discovering the gentle way Liza and Annie fall in love makes me miss Shanti more. It's why I've neglected the story. I'm afraid to know how it ends. Do they break up like Shanti and I did, or will they get their happy ending? Seventeen isn't too young to fall in love. My parents fell in love when my dad was fifteen and my mom fourteen.

The lock on the hotel door beeps, and I don't have time to clean up my sorry ass and wash away the remnants of tears before Jaya enters the room. She takes one look at me curled up with too many pillows and the comforter partially suffocating me, and her hands fall to her hips, untethered annoyance clear on her face.

"For real? Unless you got the flu in the last three hours, there's not a good enough reason to be looking like . . ." she paused, gesturing to me with one hand, clearly fighting to find the words. "That."

     LINE DRIVE TO LOVE

Calling me out doesn't help whatsoever, and my exhausted eyes well up with fresh tears. God, I should have gone to bed hours ago, it'd have been better than wallowing in self-pity.

"Sheesh, Rory, you make it extremely hard for me to stay pissed when you look like someone kicked your puppy."

A cross between a laugh and a sob escapes me. "I don't have a puppy."

"Move over, sadness." The covers get pulled back, and then Jaya is yanking the pillows away so she can slide in. Irritability from the past week lingers in her brown eyes, but I'm grateful for the effort.

"This doesn't mean I'm not still salty about you being an ass to the team."

I sniffle, "Noted."

It's silent in the dimly lit room for a long time, before I say something I've only been obsessively thinking of for the past six days.

"I–I think I made a mistake, Jay."

I expect her to ask for more details, or get testy

all over again, or pretend I'm not talking about Shanti. Instead, she says the last thing I'm expecting.

"Finally!" A pillow hits me in the face. "It's about time. Now tell me, what are you gonna do to fix it?"

21 The Final Pitch

OUR TEAM PLAYED HARD, but in the end only placed second in the championships. I thought losing would be the end all for me, but it wasn't. In fact, it didn't come close to losing Shanti. I'd built the championships, and the idea of needing to succeed in that before gaining a scholarship, up in my head for so long that winning was the only acceptable outcome. I didn't anticipate only a mild disappointment fluttering through me before reconciling with Shanti became front and centre again.

Now the bed and breakfast looms in view as I amble down Fitzroy Street, its brass lion door knocker over iron black paint in the entrance more intimidating with each step. My hands are sweaty like they were the first time I came here, but for entirely different reasons.

What if she slams the door in my face? What if I don't get a second chance? What if —

"Stop," I chide, shaking my head as if that's enough to loosen the lingering self-doubt. Drawing in a deep, steadying breath, I wipe my hands on my shirt before gripping the book tucked under my arm. It's gift wrapped now, its pages filled with annotations where I left questions or had underlined favourite passages. I hope Shanti can forgive the minor alterations in the paperback, but more than anything, I hope she's in a forgiving mood when it comes to *me*.

"You can do this," I whisper, and as I ring the doorbell, I'm hyper-aware of the rapid pulse exploding in my throat. A moment later, the front door opens and it's no longer the house looming over me, this time it's Mr. Devi. The edges of his mouth slant down as he frowns.

"Rory. This is a surprise."

Not a good one, judging by the suspicious narrowing of his brown eyes behind his glasses. I swallow, but my spit goes down wrong and I cough. My cheeks are flaming as I choke out meekly, "Hi, Mr. Devi, is Shanti here?" I hadn't called or texted, too afraid Shanti wouldn't reply. I spent most of the plane ride rereading parts of the book so that I could jot down notes, so certain a chance to connect with Shanti over *Annie on My Mind* was the way to her heart. Then, on the drive home from the airport, Jay insisted on rehearsing with me what I planned to say. Not that it did any good, considering my mind is blank under the pressure of her grandfather's gaze.

"I'm afraid Shanti is unavailable for the foreseeable future. Best of luck, Rory." Mr. Devi begins to close the door.

"Wait!" I exclaim, lurching forward to jab my foot in the threshold. I can't think past the squeezing in my chest and my heart is thundering so loud I'm sure he can hear it. "I-I'm sorry for ever hurting her. I just . . . I need to explain, to apologize, I . . ." I trail off, swallowing past the lump in my throat. I hold the book out to him, shrugging helplessly. "Can you please just give this to Shanti? I know she's upset, and I — I'll just leave things up to her."

Raindrops wash my tears away on the walk home, the late summer humidity only adding to the sickening churn in my stomach. I was stupid to think I'd be allowed in to talk to Shanti. After what I did, who could blame Mr. Devi for turning me away?

"I'm sorry I couldn't bring home gold, Pa," I murmur, keeping my gaze on our entwined hands over his bed sheets. It's just after seven, but he dozed off enough times in his chair that Mom put him to bed early. I can feel his eyes on me behind the ventilator mask, those deep pools of blue threatening to drown me if I look. I squirm under the attention, toying with the hole in my pyjama pants with the fingers not holding his. "I um, I gave it my all, you know. Char pitched some to give me a break but . . . well I think I could still have a chance to make provincials next year."

Tryouts for next year's U19 Whitecaps are being held in Charlottetown in a few weeks. Jaya and I are planning to stay down there for the weekend, and during the tryouts, hopefully, she can get a good video of me that I can use when applying to university.

"W-Whoawee . . ."

"Pa?"

When I glance over, his mask is fogging slightly as he tries again to speak. I jump from my chair. "Hold on, let me help."

I press the incline on the bed, watching as it slowly raises his head a few notches more. Then I carefully unbuckle the strap on the mask covering his mouth. His breathing is terrible when he's in bed, so we'll have to be quick. I smile, though it's been more difficult lately to keep pretending everything is okay. That *I'm* okay. "Were you saying something?"

"Jus wan . . . you happy, Whoawee." His blue eyes glistened now, pride and love shining through the wetness. "Love you."

"Love you too, Pa." My words sound husky, like I've caught a cold, and that familiar ache in my chest is back. Bending to kiss his cheek, my lips come away damp from his tears. I put the ventilator mask on again, and am grateful when he falls asleep within minutes.

I'm watching some of the footage from this weekend's game when the door to the den opens. Expecting to see Mom, I almost fall off my chair at the sight of Shanti standing there. She's wearing a grey and red graphic print boho sleeveless summer dress with a crew neckline, her beauty literally stealing my next breath. Her long black curls are loosely tousled, reaching just past her shoulders. She looks like she's on her way to dinner or a party, and it takes me a moment to notice the book clutched in her hands.

"H-hi," I stammer, crossing the room to her in three strides. My hands are shaking, so I tuck them under my arms, a little self-consciously. "You're here."

Shanti's mouth tugs up at the corners, but she glances past me to my father's bed. "How is he?"

"Oh, you know." I shrug, looking as well. "The same, really."

"Can we talk?"

"Us, or you and Pa?" At the arch of Shanti's brow, a tense chuckle escapes me. "Sorry, yes, follow me."

We pass Mom on the way up to my room, blushing as she not so subtly reminds us of her open-door policy.

"Sorry she's so cringe," I mutter, finding it hard to make eye contact as Shanti and I enter my bedroom. The door is ajar, but the room is so small the only place to sit is on the bed.

"I can't believe you actually read it," Shanti says after a stretch of silence.

I crack a small grin, and pleasure from the blatant approval in her tone torpedoes through me. I puff out my cheeks. "I said I would."

"I remember."

Shanti bites her plump bottom lip, her brown

gaze darting to me before glancing around the room. I hold my breath, shoving my hands under my thighs so I don't spontaneously throw myself at her. The floral scent on her skin is both comforting and arousing, and I'm torn between wanting to sit back and inhale her like a good gentlewoman or bury my face where her hairline ends and her neck begins.

"What, um," my brain fizzes out, and for several heartbeats, my eyes fix on her bottom lip. A gush of air leaves me, loud enough that she offers a bemused smile. "I never asked what you loved about it. I'm guessing you read the notes I left?"

Shanti nods, placing her hand on my arm and finally putting me out of my misery when she releases her lip. "I love the story for the same reasons. Their love story is sad yet so beautiful, especially for being written more than thirty years ago." She squeezes my arm, looking at me under long lashes. "*Annie on My Mind* helped me accept myself."

"I'm glad," I whisper, pulling my hand out from under me. I tentatively reach for her, skimming my thumb over her bottom lip. "I really miss you, Shanti. And I'm sorry. So, *so*, sorry. Do you think we could . . . ?"

"Yes!"

Laughter fills the room as Shanti tackles me to the mattress. Her arms come around my waist, her breasts pushed against my chest as she smothers me in kisses. I can't stop touching her either. The week and a half without her was the longest of my life. My fingers trail up her arms before sinking into the soft tendrils of her hair. Her lips lock onto mine in a passionate kiss that has my toes curling. I'm dazed when we finally pull apart, only for her to murmur, "No more being stupid, okay? Because I love you."

"I . . . you do?" I can't hold back my sappy smile, and a delirious, contented sigh slips out. Our foreheads touch. "'Cause I'm so in love with you, Shanti."

"I really do." She bites her lip, her eyes dancing with mischief as her fingers slip under the hem of my t-shirt. "How likely is it that your mom will come check on us?"

Knowing Mom is parked beside my dad's bed for the night, I grin. "Not very, if we're quiet."

Shanti winks, leaning in to kiss me again. "You're on, Taylor."

EPILOGUE
Home Run

"YOU GET YOUR HEIGHT FROM YOUR PA," Mom comments as I place the star on top of the six-foot Christmas tree Carlos and I picked out yesterday. I stand back, wrapping my arm around Mom's shoulders and give her a minute. Decorating the tree without Dad's help is always emotional. I'm sure it's hard on him as well, as all he can do is watch from his wheelchair. Always a spectator, never a player.

I grab a stray piece of garland off the floor and

head his way. "You're lookin' joyous now, Pa." I laugh, draping the garland loosely around his neck.

"Fun-ny," he groans, but I can see the smile in his gaze.

"What time is the team showing up tonight?" Mom asks, beside us now. She fusses with Dad's blanket.

A lot has happened since the summer ended. Shanti went home with more confidence to start networking her novel. She even let me read the first chapter, so, progress! Dad's been hanging in there, his disease making it harder to talk every day. He spends most of his waking hours now on the ventilator, but I swear nothing can bring his spirit down.

And I made it back onto the Whitecaps provincial softball team. It's been my goal since the second I was replaced, but now, playing softball isn't my sole focus anymore. The winter conditioning will start soon, and it might take up more time than I want to give. It's becoming clearer every day that I want to be here for my dad as long as possible. It's for that reason that I've decided to hold off on university next year. I still want the scholarship, and I'll work my ass off to get it, but leaving the island is the last thing I want right now. Dad's doctor has given him another year, maybe two, but nothing is guaranteed.

"Jaya said she'd be here around six." Yes, Jaya made the team too. I was stoked about that, and I think she only tried out so she could rub it in Neallie's face that she was good enough. It also gives me a travel buddy, since I still don't know many of the other players. We have a lot of off-island games, but thankfully it only takes me from home for a week at most.

"And Carlos is coming?"

I nod, heading over to gather up the empty boxes. "He's bringing Pascal. It'll be a full house. Are you sure you guys are okay hosting a team dinner?"

"It's a Christmas dinner, and yes, love." Mom smiles. "We just love seeing you happy, Ror."

"I really am, Ma." I smile too, my thoughts drifting to Shanti. It's been hard doing a long-distance relationship, but she's planning to apply for UPEI instead of Simon Fraser, stating that the most important thing to her is that she's with me. I couldn't agree more.

Mom takes Dad to the den for a nap, and I head upstairs to get ready for dinner. It'll be the first time I've had the entire team and my friends under this small house, but I've decided I don't care. If it's not up to their standards, they can always turn around and walk back out, or better yet, not come in at all. Jaya and I have a bet going to see whether or not Neallie does just that. It's whatev.

I'm cleaning the bathroom when Jaya, Carlos, and Pascal arrive, and I can hear them chatting in the kitchen with my mom. Ma puts everyone at ease, and I can already picture her shoving a plate of cookies at them.

"Hey, superstar," Jaya greets me as I enter the kitchen. She nudges my shoulder as I walk past to the fridge.

"Superstar?" I echo.

"Yeah, now that you're a provincial pitcher."

Like I said, a *lot* has happened. I snicker, placing a jug of milk on the table before going back for glasses, "Just a quarter of the time, remember?"

Unlike with a club team, Neallie isn't allowed to hog the mound. The Whitecaps have four regular pitchers, and I'm actually pleased with that. It gives me time to play shortstop, which I also love.

"Take the win, bro," Carlos says, his fist already hovering in the air as I sit down. I bump it, laughing.

"For sure."

Two hours later the dinner party has come and gone, everyone leaving with full bellies and gifts from our Secret Santa exchange. Carlos and Pascal left about ten minutes ago, so now only Jaya remains, helping Mom and I clean up. I'm pushing the broom down the hallway when the doorbell rings.

"Forget something?" Assuming it's Carlos, I pull open the door.

A gust of mid-December chill hits me, and I gawk at the person standing on my doorstep wearing the cutest knitted coat and toque. "Shanti. Ohmygod!

What are you doing here?" I drag her inside, shutting the door behind her.

"Surprise!" Grabbing my face with two freezing gloved hands, Shanti gives me a long kiss. When she comes up for air a wide smile breaks out across her face. "So remember when I said Mom and Dad are probably divorcing?"

Dumbfounded, I just nod.

"I was right. And guess what else? Mom and I are moving to PEI!"

"Babe, are you for real right now?" I exclaim, and my girlish squeal has us both laughing. I didn't even know my voice could *do* that.

"So real, Ror. I'll be in Charlottetown, but so much closer to you. Her job starts in January, but she let me come early so I could be with you for Christmas."

"I can't believe this." I shake my head in shock and awe. I don't know if we'll be together forever, but I hope so.

As I pull her into my arms again, it sure as hell feels like I've hit the biggest home run of my life.

THE PLAYLISTS

Rory's Playlist

- "Rainy Days and Mondays" — Carpenters
- "Dream a Little Dream of Me" — The Mamas & the Papas
- "Cry Baby" — Janis Joplin
- "That's All Right" — Elvis Presley
- "We've Only Just Begun" — Carpenters, Royal Philharmonic Orchestra
- "My Baby's Good to Me" — Fleetwood Mac
- "Ain't No Mountain High Enough" — Marvin Gaye, Tammi Terrell
- "Jackson" — Johnny Cash, June Carter-Cash
- "You're No Good" — Linda Ronstadt
- "Superstar" — Carpenters
- "I Wanna Be Where You Are" — Michael Jackson
- "You Can't Always Get What You Want" — The Rolling Stones
- "You're So Vain" — Carly Simon
- "Dancing Queen" — ABBA
- "Almost Always True" — Elvis Presley
- "Mrs. Robinson" — Simon and Garfunkel
- "It's Too Late" — Carole King
- "Dreams" (2004 Remaster) — Fleetwood Mac
- "Bennie and the Jets" — Elton John
- "Comfortably Numb" — Pink Floyd
- "Rhiannon" — Fleetwood Mac
- "Rock with You" — Michael Jackson
- "Girlfriend" — Michael Jackson
- "Keep On Going" — Fleetwood Mac
- "Leaving on a Jet Plane" — Peter, Paul, and Mary

* "Maybe" — Janis Joplin
* "Suspicious Minds" — Elvis Presley
* "So Far Away" — Carole King
* "Dedicated to the One I Love" — The Mamas & the Papas

Shanti's Playlist

* "girls, girls, girls" — FLETCHER
* "Why Am I Like This?" — The World Alive
* "Favorite Sin" — Ash Morgan
* "Wait a Minute!" — Willow
* "One of Us" — The World Alive, Bad Omens
* "Forever" — FLETCHER
* "we fell in love in october" — girl in red
* "Just Pretend" — Bad Omens
* "In Your Love" — Tyler Childers
* "Gemini Moon" — Reneé Rapp
* "THE DEATH OF PEACE AND MIND" — Bad Omens
* "Wildest Dreams" — Taylor Swift
* "Becky's So Hot" — FLETCHER
* "Miss Your Face" — Too Close To Touch
* "Hi." — Lauren Sanderson
* "Like a Villain" — Bad Omens
* "Daughter" — L Devine
* "Not Strong Enough" — boygenius
* "Pretending" — FLETCHER
* "Be Your Man" — G Flip
* "Lady May" — Tyler Childers
* "If I Loved a Boy" — We Three
* "Watermelon Sugar" — Harry Styles
* "Delicate" — Taylor Swift

ACKNOWLEDGEMENTS

There are so many people to thank, but truly, the softball in this romance I've created wouldn't be half as good without the help of Coach C. Thank you for always being chipper, even when I asked a gazillion questions and then asked them again (repeatedly) when my brain just wouldn't process. I swear learning the ins and outs of softball is the equivalent of learning a new language.

Thank you to my wonderful beta readers: Amber, Paige, Ava, Meghan, Sarah, and Coach C. You believed in the story and helped me polish it to the best version possible. I appreciate you all for the endless support and guidance.

Thank you to Lorimer for taking me on again. It's always such a fun learning experience, and for Rory's story especially, I'm glad you helped me steer it in a different direction.

A special thanks to Allister for loving and believing in this story. You're a great editor, and I'm so glad you're in my corner!

Last but not least, thank you to my wife and kids. You guys are always ready to go on a fictional adventure with me, and it means more than you can possibly imagine. I love you all!

Until the next one,

Angel

AUTHOR'S NOTE

Wow, I can't believe Rory and Shanti are finally out in the world! What a whirlwind year it's been, getting Line Drive to Love from thought to paperback. I'll be honest, though I've appreciated softball from afar, I can't recall ever going to a game. Certainly not watching Facebook clips of college softball games! I researched the crap out of this book because I wanted to go through the motions with Rory, and I'm so glad I did. Rory Taylor is an old soul with big dreams and an even bigger heart. I loved getting to know her, her besties, her parents, and, of course, her love, Shanti. It was an honour to write Rory's story, and I can only hope it touches a lot of readers.